JESSICA BECK
THE DONUT MYSTERIES, BOOK 55
DONUT HEARTS HOMI-CIDE

The First Time Ever Published!
The 55th Donuts Mystery!
DONUT HEARTS HOMICIDE

Jessica Beck is the *New York Times* Bestselling Author of the Donut Mysteries, the Cast Iron Cooking Mysteries, the Classic Diner Mysteries, and the Ghost Cat Cozy Mysteries.

THERE'S A VALENTINE'S Day scavenger hunt in April Springs, and Donut Hearts is one of the stops. Couples go from place to place and post photos of themselves together as they solve puzzles that lead them to the next venue. The grand prize is a romantic weekend in Asheville, but the contest gets shut down prematurely when one of the players is murdered during the hunt! Suzanne and Trish must find the killer before someone else loses more than just the game!

To P and E,
For always believing!
And to all of my loyal readers,
For helping make my dreams come true!

Chapter 1

I HONESTLY THOUGHT the Valentine's Day scavenger hunt was a good idea when I first heard about it. After all, foot traffic at my donut shop was lagging a bit due to the run of bad weather we'd been having since early January, and I figured the exposure would be good for *all* of the merchants of downtown April Springs, not just me.

Unfortunately, what started off as a fun experience for the town turned out to be deadly for one of our residents, and Jake and I had to find the killer before they could strike again.

But I'm getting ahead of myself, as usual. My name's Suzanne Hart, and my shop is aptly named Donut Hearts. My place was a perfect match for a Valentine scavenger hunt, and I had a brand-new heart-shaped donut cutter I was dying to try out.

If only things had turned out to be that innocent in the end.

"Suzanne, are you prepared for the barbarians to pillage and plunder our shops?" Gabby Williams asked me as she looked around Donut Hearts on Valentine's Day, the day of the planned townwide scavenger hunt. Gabby was finally getting over what had happened to her during her ill-fated and rather short-lived marriage, and I was glad to see a bit of spirit back in her, even though it meant that her biting wit had returned in full force as well.

"Bring them on," I said with a grin as I pointed to the nearby overflowing table, situated mostly out of sight from the front window. The display had temporarily replaced over half of my regular seating, but I'd needed that much room to offer plates loaded with over a dozen plain cake donuts cut into two half circles, as well as red, pink, and white icing, three kinds of heart-shaped sprinkles, and half a dozen other decorating extras to boot. "I'm ready for them, if any of the contestants actually figure out enough clues to make it here," I told her. "How about you?"

"I suppose I'm as ready as I'll ever be," she said with a hint of exasperation in her voice. "I'm still not sure I like the idea of the town's riffraff pawing through my things."

"Come on, Gabby. You get to be a part of a scavenger hunt on Valentine's Day. At least yours isn't going to be messy like mine is sure to be."

My friend looked at me for a moment, and then she smiled, something that was nice to see from her again after such a long drought of happiness. "We do go through a great deal for our town, don't we? How did we let the mayor talk us into this?"

"Honestly, it was more at Samantha's urging than George's," I said. "Everyone knows that she's the power behind the throne these days."

"For the moment, at any rate," Gabby said cryptically.

"Why do you say that? Do you know something I don't?" I asked her.

"I'm sure I know a great *many* somethings you are unaware of," Gabby answered, but her soft smile took any sting out of her comment. "But I understand the mayor's restaurateur girlfriend isn't too pleased with his new assistant, so something is bound to have to change on that front."

"Why would Angelica DeAngelis care about Samantha Peterson? Angelica is a force all her own. Surely she's not jealous of *Samantha*. Everyone knows that George is crazy about Angelica." My friend was the owner of nearby Union Square's Napoli's—the best Italian restaurant in ten counties— and she was not only a stunning woman, with four grown daughters nearly as lovely as she, but she was also one of the sweetest people I knew as well.

"I'm afraid it's not the mayor's affections Samantha craves; it's his job," Gabby explained.

"Seriously? But *George* is our mayor," I protested.

"He is at the moment, and he generally does a fine job of it, though if you tell him I said that, I'll patently deny it. That being said, some folks are saying that since he started dating Ms. DeAngelis, his heart isn't in his job anymore. I don't mean me, but some people," she added quickly. Gabby knew I was a staunch supporter and friend of our mayor, and though most folks in April Springs wouldn't go toe-to-toe with her about anything short of life and death, she wasn't all that keen to cross me either, at least not normally.

"If she's such a threat, then why doesn't he just fire her?" I asked. "It's not like George doesn't burn through his assistants at an alarming rate anyway. What's one more?"

"Most of the ladies from the past have been more interested in the man than they were in the job. This is different," Gabby said. "Anyway, I didn't come here to gossip about the goings-on in city hall. I just wanted to make sure you were set up and ready for the onslaught."

"I am, at least as much as I can be," I said with a shrug, still miffed about Samantha daring to go against her boss. "Where do you think the first contestants are by now?" I asked as I studied the large confidential map of locations we'd each been given just before the contest had begun. There were large red hearts around my shop, Gabby's business, Paige's bookstore, Trish's diner, Cutnip hair salon, the town clock, the gazebo in the park near the cottage I shared with my husband, and, finally, city hall itself. The clue leading to the donut shop had been fun to read since we'd all gotten a sneak peek that morning of the riddle that led to our individual locations, and of course we could always cheat and read the one that led to the next stage of the competition hidden at our shops, which I was dead certain all of us did the second Samantha dropped them off. I'd marveled at her creativity in coming up with the clues, even if they did give the answers away pretty much at first glance. She probably had to do it that way to make it easy for the contestants to move on to the next stage of the competition.

The one leading to Donut Hearts read,

"For a sinful taste,
It's time for haste.

You should Love the name,
If you enjoy this game."

Hearts was a Valentine's name if ever there was one, synonymous with love. That clue was at the town clock, split in half and taped under two matching fake rocks at its base, hidden among a large collection of jumbled stones brought in just for the contest. The clue they got at my place was taped under a chocolate-hued cast iron donut I would be holding in my hands. I'd found a set of three at an antique shop in Asheville, decorated individually in pastels of vanilla, rich chocolate, and creamy strawberry, each sporting colorful sprinkles as well. The set had cost a small fortune, at least a small fortune for me, but I'd had to own them. Apparently I was a woman of singular taste. I had all three of them on my display counter at the moment, smiling inwardly that no one would have any idea that one of the donuts held their next clue until I showed it to them.

"Grab your Grill,
Where you get your fill.
We'll give you a tip,
Some of its offerings flip."

That led across the street to the Boxcar Grill, where I knew that a stack of old menus was piled up on a table in back of the diner. I wasn't sure how Trish had planned to make them match, but I knew that the contestants had to find the two halves, take a photo of themselves with the reunited pair with their cell phones, and then send it to city hall. That was something they had to do at every stop along the way as they accomplished each task to prove that they hadn't skipped any steps, including selfie shots with their decorated donut halves, reunited with icing and adorned with extras.

The final destination was city hall, where the mayor and his assistant were waiting for the winners to arrive. The first couple that cracked every riddle and sent their photos along the way won a weekend trip to a romantic inn in the mountains of North Carolina. I kind of wished

Jake and I could have played. It really sounded like fun, and I could surely use a weekend away, especially if it was all expenses paid.

Whoever won would earn it, though.

"What number are you on the list of clues?" I asked Gabby.

"I'm right after Cutnip, something I resent on principle alone," she complained. "Look, the first contestants are leaving the bookstore," Gabby said as she pointed across the street toward The Last Page. "The way they have to zigzag all up and down Springs Drive is insane."

"Well, they couldn't exactly put them in order of proximity, could they? That would make for a short competition," I said as I watched couples stream out of the bookstore, looking determined to make their way to the hair salon down the street.

Gabby asked me, "What did Paige do for her matching pairs for the contestants?"

"She wanted to use writers who were couples in real life like Mary and Percy Shelley, but I convinced her that most folks weren't nearly as literate as she is. Besides, those two didn't exactly enjoy a romantic love story in real life. Instead, Paige created a pile of romance novels with two different books by the same author. The contestants have to match the author name, take their photo, and present the books to Paige to get their next clue. She wasn't supposed to tell me, but she said they are going to Cutnip from there, but I don't know what they're doing to make a match."

"I understand it has something to do with a bucket of hair curlers, but what they are going to do with those is beyond me," she said, shaking her head. "Whatever they do, I'm willing to bet that it won't be very dignified. My location riddle is there."

"What does yours say?"

"You'll have to try on a few,
To tell the old from the NEW.
The fit must be right,
Or you'll never take flight."

"It's cute," I said.

"I suppose," Gabby allowed. "I taped the next clue on the sole of a slipper I held out just for that purpose." She glanced at my clock and added, "I'd better get back to my shop. No one, and I mean no one, is going to ransack my place of business, contest or no contest."

"How are they supposed to find matching shoes, then?" I asked her.

"It should be easy enough to do," she replied. "I made a pile of all kinds of shoes in a single area in front of the shop, so at least the chaos will be a bit contained there. They have to bring me a pair of shoes, any pair from the pile, take their photos, each holding one shoe, and then I show them their next clue. Nice and neat; no fuss, no muss."

I didn't think there was much chance of that with folks rushing around like mad, but that was one argument I didn't care to have with her. If Gabby thought she could keep the contestants in check, more power to her. I myself was resigned to cleaning up after the mob, and besides, it would be fun watching them decorate their donuts and marry the pieces together with icing. My assistant, Emma, was participating in the contest along with her boyfriend, locally renowned chef Barton Gleason, so I planned to pull up one of the last remaining chairs and watch the entire thing by myself as I guarded the cast iron donut with the next clue. Once they decorated their donuts and took their photos as proof, I'd show them their next clue, so at least I'd have a little fun in the process. I'd invited Jake to join me, but he was on his way to Raleigh. Evidently his sister was having yet more problems with the men in her life, and Jake was going to help her pick up the pieces of her shattered love life.

Still, it would be nice for me to see who was paired up in the great scavenger hunt and watch them as they made their way through my task.

At least I hoped it would be worth the mess they were sure to leave in their wake.

To my surprise, Samantha Peterson herself came into the shop first with a timid little man following her as he carried an official-looking clipboard. I knew him by sight, but to my knowledge, he'd never been in my donut shop, at least not while I'd been there. That was entirely possible these days, since Emma and her mother, Sharon, ran Donut Hearts two days a week in my stead.

Samantha was a nice-looking woman in her late forties, with short jet-black hair and piercing green eyes that reminded me of a cat. She was a curvy woman like me, but I always look a bit heavier than I should, while her pounds had been distributed perfectly. She must have been beautiful when she smiled, but I couldn't say, since I'd never seen her show one.

Samantha glanced at my table and sniffed the air. "Is that *all* of the decorations you have?"

She made it sound a bit like an accusation, as though I were holding out bags and bags of sprinkles and frosting in back that I reserved for my real customers.

"That's the best Donut Hearts has to offer," I told her. "Was there something I could help you with?" I asked, trying to keep a smile on my face, though at the moment, it was a bit difficult.

"I'm just going around making sure that everything is in place, and Gray is checking the locations off his list."

Gray Blackhurst offered me a faint smile as he glanced up from his clipboard and then immediately back down to it.

"You can check me off, then," I told him.

Evidently, Samantha didn't like anyone else talking to her assistant. "When *I* am satisfied that it is right, then *I* will instruct him to do so, and not a moment sooner."

Okay, then, so much for pleasantries. "Knock yourself out," I said as a lone customer came into the shop.

"Do you have any fritters left? I've been craving cherry all morning," the man said.

"Where is your partner?" Samantha asked him pointedly.

The man looked around the shop, clearly confused. "You sell *donuts* here, right? Do I have to have a girlfriend or wife to buy one?"

"Of course you don't," I said as I moved behind the counter. "You're in luck. I normally don't make cherry fritters, but in honor of the day, I decided to offer them today."

"What, Tuesday?" he asked, still befuddled by the responses he was getting in my shop.

"Yes, it's Tuesday, but it's also Valentine's Day," I said.

A look of sheer horror crossed his face. "*It's Valentine's Day?* My wife is going to kill me. I bet there's not a flower shop with anything left in it in the entire state by now."

"Might I suggest a dozen assorted donuts?" I offered. "She might like those more than flowers."

"Knowing her, she just might," he said. "Box them up, and put a few fritters in a bag, too."

As I did as he asked, Samantha asked, "Can't your assistant handle that?"

"She could if she were here," I said, "but she's not, so she can't."

Samantha shook her head slightly, showing her disapproval, but I didn't care.

After I told the man how much his treats cost, he asked, "You don't happen to have any cards, do you?"

"Like To and From?" I asked him.

"No, more like a greeting card," he corrected me.

"Try the bookstore across the street," I said as I pointed to The Last Page. "Paige might have something there."

"Thanks. You're a lifesaver," he told me as he took his change, grabbed his goodies, and then hurried out the door.

"I trust that won't happen while the contestants are here," Samantha said huffily.

"Funny, I hope just the opposite. This is still a viable business, you know," I answered with a sweet smile. "Samantha, should you really be seen visiting the spots on the scavenger hunt? It kind of gives it away, doesn't it?"

Gray looked up and suppressed a quick smile, but not before I saw it. Samantha didn't answer. She just stared at me for a moment then turned to the door. "Come, Gray."

Once the hunt organizer was gone, I let out a deep breath I hadn't realized I'd been holding in. There was something about that woman I didn't like. Maybe it was because she was going after George's job, but it could have been because she was a bit too pushy, a little too abrupt to suit my taste. After all, I ran a donut shop, a laid-back and easygoing business if ever there was one, at least when I was working the front counter. I liked to see smiles on the people who visited my shop, not frowns.

I did my best to drive any thoughts of the woman out of my mind and focused on the couples who would be joining me at Donut Hearts soon enough. I found myself wishing that my placement had been earlier in the hunt so I could have the shop cleaned up by now, but I hadn't been given any choice in the matter, and it was hard to say why Samantha had chosen the order she had.

While I waited for contestants to arrive, I sold a few donuts, ate one myself if I'm being honest about it, and did a bit of light cleaning until the first pair showed up.

When they did, it certainly wasn't the type of couple I'd been expecting.

Chapter 2

"WHAT CAN I GET YOU, gentlemen?" I asked as Thompson Smythe walked in with Gunther Peale on his heels.

"We're here for the contest," Thompson said gruffly.

"You two are a *couple*? Not that there's anything wrong with that," I added quickly. The two old-timers weren't exactly emblematic of young love in any way, shape, or form. Thompson was a retired attorney, always impeccably dressed, while Gunther had been a stonemason his entire adult life. He had beefy shoulders and large, weathered hands that looked powerful enough to squeeze blocks and stones into submission.

"Why not? We lost our wives, and we couldn't get dates," Gunther explained. "Besides, if we both brought women with us, things might get complicated."

"And you two want to go together to a romantic getaway?" I asked. "I had no idea you were dating."

"Dating? Are you out of your mind? I'm not dating him," Thompson said, clearly outraged by the very idea.

"Hey, you could do worse," Gunther said, clearly offended by his partner's vehement denial, no doubt.

"We're selling it online when we win," Thompson said. "That was the agreement."

"Yeah, I wanted to talk to you about that," Gunther said.

Thompson grunted. "There is nothing to talk about. We agreed to sell the weekend, so that's what we're going to do, and that's final."

"Are you sure there's not a rule against you doing that?" I asked the men.

"Nope. We checked the rules, and don't forget, old Mr. Whiskers here used to be a lawyer. He went through the details with a fine-toothed comb," Gunther explained with a twinkle in his eye.

"Maybe so, but is it *ethical*?" I asked him.

"It's not a question of ethics. Rules are rules, and they must be followed," Thompson said. He noticed his companion grinning. "What are you smiling about?"

"She just asked a lawyer about ethics," he explained.

"Stop yakking and start decorating," Thompson answered.

I wasn't sure about their motivation, but thankfully, I wasn't in charge of the contest. After they decorated two donut halves and got their photos taken, Thompson said, "Next clue, please."

I turned the donut over in my hand and showed them.

"Let's go," Gunther said as he headed out the door.

"Do we get to keep these?" Thompson asked as he pointed to the plate with their decorated donut.

"Of course," I replied. "Why, do you want a keepsake?"

"No, I want a snack," he said, and then he took a bite of donut. Almost immediately, he spat it back out onto his plate. "Too sweet."

"Is that someone going into the Boxcar?" I asked, pretending to see something, though I hadn't.

"Come on. You're holding us up," Gunther said as he left without Thompson.

"I'm coming, you old fool," the attorney answered.

"It takes one to know one," I heard Gunther say as the door closed.

They were still bickering as they crossed the street, but they weren't my problem anymore.

I turned to see a new couple arrive, one that was slightly less disconcerting than the last one but not by much.

It was our new doctor, Zoey Hicks, accompanied by Luke Davenport, a local man who had recently won a chunk of money in the lottery and was doing his best to blow his way through it in record time. Luke had helped Grace and me after a car accident we'd had quite a while ago, but we normally didn't run in the same circles.

"Suzanne, how lovely your shop looks," Zoey said. She turned to her companion. "Doesn't it, Luke?"

"Lovely," he mimicked, though it was clear his heart wasn't in the scavenger hunt. "I still think this is a bad idea, Zoey. I don't want to run into Samantha," he added as they hastily finished their donuts and married them together.

The young doctor put a hand on his shoulder and looked directly into his eyes. "Luke, that is old news. You are with me now."

"It's not *that* old," he said in mild protest.

"Would you rather be with her?" Zoey asked, the chill strong in her voice.

"No. No. Of course not. I'm just saying," he protested mildly. "She's going to cause a scene when we show up at city hall."

Zoey patted his cheek a few times. "Let me worry about her, Luke. I can handle the likes of Samantha Peterson." She then turned to me. "Where is the next clue, Suzanne?"

I held up the donut and showed her.

"Clever," she said and then turned to Luke. "Come on. We're close. I can feel it."

"Coming," he said docilely.

The mayor popped in during a rush of donut decorators, and as I got him an old-fashioned donut and a cup of coffee, I said, "I thought you'd be at city hall, waiting for the first arrivals."

"I was, but Samantha had things under control there, so I decided to stretch my legs for a bit."

"George, I'm surprised you and Angelica aren't taking part in the contest."

He shrugged. "Why? We both make a good living. If we want to get away, we can afford to pay the going rate."

"How are things going?" I asked him as I gave him his change.

"With my job or my love life?" he asked me a little grumpily.

"Both. Either. Or. You pick."

"Everything's fine," he said in a tone that told me he clearly didn't want to talk about it.

I decided to take him at his word, even though I knew he was lying. "Good to hear. You know we all have your back, right?"

He started to say something but then reconsidered. "Thanks, Suzanne."

"You're welcome. You know the rules: free moral support with every purchase here at Donut Hearts."

He barely smiled, and then Mayor Morris was gone. Something was clearly weighing on his mind, but he hadn't wanted to talk about it, and I didn't have time to grill him. After the scavenger hunt was finished, though, I planned to track him down and have a heart-to-heart conversation with him.

In the meantime, I had work to do making sure that my part of the event went well.

Several couples came in and out of Donut Hearts over the next half hour, decorating donuts in a mad frenzy before heading over to the Boxcar Grill.

Emma and Barton finally came in, both looking a bit worse for the wear.

"Where have you two been?" I asked her.

"*Somebody* wouldn't leave his kitchen," Emma said, looking at Barton.

"Emma, I'm trying to perfect a new recipe," he protested. "These things can't be rushed."

"Don't you want a romantic weekend away with me?" Emma asked him.

"Honestly, even if we win, I'm not sure I'll be able to spare the time."

"Then maybe I'll have to take someone else," she said softly.

"Come on, Emma. Don't be that way."

"Be what way? I'm just saying," she answered, her voice trailing off.

"I'll do better. I promise."

"I'm sorry, but you'll have to prove it," she told him.

Then, to my surprise as much as Emma's, Barton took her shoulders and gave her a kiss that no doubt rocked her back on her feet. When he finally broke away, he asked, "How was that?"

"Better, but there's still room for improvement," my assistant answered with a twinkle in her eyes.

"I could try again, but Suzanne might throw us out," Barton replied with a sheepish grin.

"Okay, but I want a rain check," Emma answered as she looked at the counter. "Where's the third one, Suzanne?"

"The third what?" I asked her.

"Cast iron donut," she answered. "The chocolate one is in your lap, and the vanilla one is on the counter, but I don't see the strawberry one."

"Blast it," I said as I jumped up from my seat and looked around. "Someone must have stolen it!"

"Oh, no. That's terrible," she answered.

"Why on earth would someone take it?" I asked, mourning the loss of the matched set. I loved those cast iron donuts, and now someone had taken one. It wasn't as though they were good for anything but paperweights. I tried to think about who had lingered over the display case where they'd been, but I'd been so wrapped up in the decorating and photo taking that I'd failed to pay attention to the entire shop. I had a feeling I'd never see the strawberry donut again, and suddenly, the Valentine's Day scavenger hunt lost quite a bit of its charm for me.

Doing my best to put on a brave face, I said, "Well, don't let that stop you from decorating your donut."

"It's not like we have a chance of winning," Emma said. "Barton, why don't you go back to the kitchen and work on that recipe?"

"What are *you* going to do if I do that?" he asked, clearly intrigued by the idea but fearful that it might be a trap. The young man was not stupid, after all.

"I'm going to help Suzanne clean up. Maybe we'll find the donut under something."

"Emma, it's your day off. You don't have to pitch in here," I protested.

"Don't have to; want to," she said. After giving Barton a quick kiss, she said, "Happy Valentine's Day. I didn't know what to get you, anyway."

"This is perfect," he said, pausing only long enough to kiss her again before bolting for the door.

"Are you sure about this?" I asked Emma after he was gone.

"Positive. When are they ending this?"

"Samantha's supposed to call us all," I told her, "but I'm not sure she will." I glanced at the door and didn't see anyone else headed our way. "I think it's time."

"We were the last of the contestants, as far as I could tell anyway," Emma said.

"Then let's clean this mess up and try to get life back to normal," I replied.

We were still working on it when the front door opened. I was hoping it wasn't another couple, but when I saw that it was our chief of police, sporting a grim look on his face, I had a hunch that what I was about to hear was going to be worse, much worse.

"Suzanne, does this look familiar?" he asked me as he held up a plastic evidence bag with the missing strawberry cast iron donut in it.

"Where did you find it? We've been looking all over for it," Emma said.

"Chief Grant, why is it in an evidence bag?" I asked, and then I looked closer at it.

It was suddenly clear that all of the coloring on it wasn't original.

Some of it had been added, and it wasn't icing.

It had to be dried blood.

Someone had evidently used one of my souvenirs as a weapon.

I just hoped that it hadn't been fatal, but there was a stirring in my gut that told me I was most likely wrong about that.

Chapter 3

"WHAT HAPPENED?" I ASKED as I stared at the paperweight.

"When was the last time you saw this?" the chief asked me, ignoring my question.

"It was on the counter this morning over by the vanilla one," I said.

"Are there just two of them?" he asked.

"No, I used the chocolate one to give folks the next clue as they finished up here," I told him, not able to take my gaze off of the donut-turned-weapon.

"I'll need the other two," he said as he held out two more evidence bags.

"The chocolate one never left my sight," I protested, but I gave them both to him anyway. "*Now* are you going to tell me what happened? That's dried blood, isn't it?"

He nodded solemnly. "It is."

"And somebody used it as a weapon," I stated matter-of-factly.

"They did."

"Come on, Chief. Give me *something*. That was my personal property used to commit the crime. Was it murder?"

"I'm afraid to say that it was," he said sadly, and then he shrugged. "You'll hear about it sooner or later, so it might as well be from me. Somebody used your cast iron donut to hit Samantha Peterson in the temple. She must have died instantly, from what Dr. Hicks told me."

"She has already seen the body?" I asked.

"As a matter of fact, she's the one who found it," he told me.

"Chief, there's something you need to know about her," I said solemnly.

"Don't tell me. You don't like her either. Grace has a problem with the woman, too. So she's smart and pretty, and isn't afraid to show off her figure a little? Does that make her a bad person?"

"It's not that. Zoey Hicks is dating Luke Davenport, who recently dumped Samantha Peterson. Evidently, there was some trouble between the three of them, and Zoey said that she'd deal with Samantha herself and told Luke not to worry about her." I hated sounding like a gossip, but the police chief needed to know.

"How do you know all of that?" he asked me.

"They were discussing it while they were here earlier, icing their donuts," I replied.

"Okay. I'll talk to her again."

"How about Luke? Was he with her when she discovered the body?" Emma asked.

I had to wonder if she was asking out of her own curiosity or if it was because of her father. Ray Blake was the sole reporter, editor, ad man, and publisher of the *April Springs Sentinel*, our hometown rag of a newspaper.

"Evidently, he went to get them something to drink."

"Where exactly was she found?" I asked.

"In the bushes behind the gazebo," he said, "but that's all I'm going to tell you. It's my turn to ask questions now. Who had access to that donut before you noticed it was missing?"

"Let's see. I can make you a list if you'd like."

"Just tell me. I'll write the names down."

"Okay, Gunther Peale and Thompson Smythe were here first, then Zoey and Luke. After that, Judge Hurley and Jenny White came in, then Bob the snowplow driver and his wife, Eunice, then there was Greg Rhyne and Mary Fran from Cutnip. After that, Terri Milner and her husband came by. Next was..."

"Was there *anyone* from town who wasn't in your shop?" the chief asked me pointedly.

"What can I say? The scavenger hunt was more popular than I thought it would be."

"Was the mayor here, by any chance?" he asked me.

"He came by for a snack in the middle of the rush," I admitted. "Come on, Chief. You don't suspect the *mayor* had anything to do with what happened, do you?"

"Suzanne, I'm just gathering facts right now," he said tersely.

"I know that look on your face, though. I've seen it before. George didn't do it," I said emphatically.

Chief Grant chose not to comment one way or the other. "Is there anyone else who was here that *wasn't* a contestant?"

"Let's see. Gabby came by first thing this morning, and then Samantha showed up with her assistant, Gray, in tow. After they left, I started getting participants in the game. Was there anyone else in particular you were interested in, or are you just asking in general?"

"I'll take whatever you've got," he said.

"Sorry, that's all I have."

"How about you?" he asked Emma. "Did you see anyone Suzanne didn't mention?"

"I just got here twenty minutes ago myself," my assistant admitted.

Chief Grant glanced at the clock. "It's a little late for coming in to work at a donut shop, isn't it?"

"Barton and I were going to do the hunt together, but since we were dead last, we decided to quit while we were behind. He headed back to the restaurant to work on a recipe, and I stayed here to help Suzanne clean up."

"Does that mean you've already wiped the counter down where the cast iron donuts were sitting?" he asked a bit glumly.

"Yes, and I thoroughly cleaned the vanilla donut, too," I admitted. "I was going to tuck them in my office where they'd be safe from thieves, so I gave them both a good cleaning first."

"I'll take them anyway," he said, though clearly some of his hopes were dashed by my admission.

"Chief, is there anything I can do to help?" I asked.

"I suppose it would be too much to ask you not to meddle in this case," he said with a resigned tone in his voice.

"Let's see. Someone chose something that I hold dear as a murder weapon, and you're asking me not to get involved? Sorry, it's not happening," I told him bluntly. There had been a time in my life when I might have lied to him, or at least not openly admitted defying his wishes, but this was personal. Someone had come into my shop, stood near me, stole one of my most valued possessions, and then used it to commit murder.

There was no way I could ever just let that go.

"I figured as much. At least you won't be able to drag Grace into this with you. She'll be out of town at that meeting for another three days," he said.

"See? There's your silver lining. Your domestic tranquility won't be affected at all."

"Who are you going to tap as your partner in this? Please don't say Jake."

"I would," I admitted, "but my husband is on his way to visit his sister in Raleigh."

"On Valentine's Day?" the chief asked me.

"We had our celebration last night," I told him. "His sister just got dumped by another jerk who didn't want to spring for flowers, candy, and a dinner out, so Jake is going there to console her and make sure she stays out of trouble." Sarah had a terrible picker when it came to the men in her life, but who was I to criticize her? I'd picked Max the first time around, and he'd cheated on me, so I wasn't one to talk. Still, she had a terrible track record when it came to men, and Jake was very overprotective of his sister.

"I can't wait to see who you rope in," he said wryly.

"Neither can I," I answered.

As the police chief headed for the door, he said, "If you think of anything or anyone else, let me know, okay?"

"Will do," I said. "Good luck."

He let that one slide, and then he was gone.

Once Chief Grant left Donut Hearts, Emma asked, "Would you like me to hang around and help you finish cleaning up?"

I glanced at the clock and saw that we were indeed past our normal closing time. I flipped the sign and locked the door. "That would be great."

"Okay," she said a bit glumly.

I couldn't keep it in. "You want to go tell your dad everything we just heard, don't you?"

"Suzanne, I promised you I'd keep him out of here, and I meant it. I don't want my father to come between us ever again."

"Neither do I," I confessed, "but you don't have to help me clean up. Go ahead," I added as I unlocked the door for her.

"You won't be mad if I tell him what I just heard?" Emma asked me.

"Hey, the police chief didn't say what he told us was in confidence." As Emma started to leave, I added, "Just keep in mind that he might not be happy about you reporting what he said to your father. I know Stephen Grant seems like a nice guy, but as chief of police, he can be a hard man. He pretty much has to be, given the job."

"I get what you're saying," Emma said after a moment. "Maybe I'll go see Barton instead."

"It's your call," I told her, even though I thought seeing her fiancé and one of her restaurant partners was an excellent idea instead of reporting to her dad, but I managed to keep it to myself.

Once Emma was gone, I went about the business of closing Donut Hearts for the day. I hadn't been that big a fan of Samantha Peterson, but that didn't mean that I approved of someone killing her so close to my donut shop and the cottage I shared with Jake. The fact that they used something of mine as a murder weapon was even worse. As I set the shop's front back in order and cleaned up, I wondered who I should ask for help, since Grace and Jake were both out of the running. I could ask Momma, but she led a very busy life, and I hated to take her away from her many business concerns. Her husband, former chief of police Phillip Martin, was a good choice, but I had no idea what he was up to at the moment. There was only one way to find out, though. I certainly had enough donuts left over from the lack of sales that day to bribe him into helping me, not that I'd need them. Phillip was always ready to dig into a case, though since he'd retired, mostly what he'd been interested in were very cold cases that were still unsolved after decades.

I boxed up nearly five dozen donuts and shut off the lights as I left the shop. As I made my way to my Jeep, I saw a flyer on the ground, fluttering in the breeze, announcing the scavenger hunt. It had been Samantha Peterson's last act on this earth, and from what I'd been able to see, it had been a successful one. I suddenly found myself wondering who had won the contest, or if they'd even declared a winner given the circumstances. I doubted the grand prize, as exclusive as it was, had been enough motive for someone to kill for though.

Not that there seemed to be a lack of suspects who might have wanted to see her come to harm.

I'd have to start a list when I recruited my partner in the job. I'd promised Jake and my mother on separate occasions not to hunt for killers on my own anymore, and so far, I'd managed to keep my word.

If Phillip couldn't help me though, I'd have to find someone else to pitch in or risk going against the two people I love most in the world.

Chapter 4

"KNOCK, KNOCK," I SAID as I rapped on Momma and Phillip's front door. I was happy to see that my mother's car was gone, while my stepfather's truck was still in the driveway. The truth of the matter was that it would be easier recruiting him to help me in my investigation if Momma was off somewhere else. It wasn't that she didn't want me to ask her husband for assistance, it was more of the fact that she worried about us both individually. Together, our partnership was probably a special kind of nightmare for her, risking the two people she cared most for in the world.

I was starting to wonder if maybe I should ask someone else when the front door opened. Phillip spotted the single box of a dozen donuts in my hands I'd carried in from the Jeep and grinned from ear to ear. "Are those for me? And here I didn't get you a thing. Happy Valentine's Day, Suzanne. Come on in."

"Thanks. The same to you. Care for a treat?"

He pretended to look around. "That depends. Do you see my wife anywhere nearby?"

"My mother, you mean?" I asked with a laugh.

"Same lady," he answered as he took the box from me. "Outstanding. What do we have here?"

"A little of this, a little of that," I admitted. "Business was kind of slow, what with the scavenger hunt and all."

"That was today, wasn't it? How did it go?" he asked before taking a bite of one of my new heart-shaped donuts I'd made using my brand-new cutter.

"You haven't heard?" I asked him as I slipped out of my coat and hung it up. "Someone killed Samantha Peterson."

"That's terrible," he said. "I hope George has an alibi."

"What makes you say that?" I asked him intently.

"Come on. Everyone knows she was gunning for him. They had an argument in city hall yesterday when I was there looking for some old records on a case I'm working on."

"Did you happen to hear what they were fighting about?" I asked.

"I didn't hear how it started, but it ended with him saying, 'If you're coming after me and my job, you'd better do it with guns blazing.' She wasn't shot, was she?"

"No," I said.

"There's at least that, then," Phillip said before sampling another donut from the box.

"The killer used one of the cast iron donuts I bought in Asheville," I told him.

"They didn't. I knew those things were heavy, but I never thought of them as deadly weapons."

"You know as well as I do that just about anything can be used to kill someone if the conditions are right," I told him.

"So this is personal now, isn't it? Do I even need to ask you if you're digging into Samantha's murder?"

"You don't. I am."

"Is Grace helping you?" he asked as he took another bite. It was almost as though he were afraid my mother would come home suddenly and take the treats away from him before he could sample each one.

"She's out of town," I answered.

"Jake then," he said, taking yet another bite from a new donut.

"He's on his way to see his sister this afternoon," I replied, frowning at the box of partially discarded donuts in his hand. "Is there something wrong with those?"

"No, they're amazing," he said as he licked two of his fingers. "Why do you ask?"

"You keep taking one bite and then putting it back," I said. "To be honest with you, it's kind of hurting my feelings."

"I didn't mean to," he said quickly. "It's something new I'm trying. I've put on a few more pounds than I'd like to lately, so instead of indulging in my favorite treats, I'm allowing myself one bite of anything I want, but only one bite."

"How's it working out for you so far?" I asked, partially mollified by his explanation.

"I've lost two pounds in four weeks," he said proudly as he put the box down. "Does that mean you came by to recruit your mother or me?"

"You're half right."

"Your mother isn't here," he said a bit sadly, "but I'm sure she'll take your call."

"I'm here for you, Phillip. What do you say? Care to join me in a little investigating?"

"Is there such a thing as a little investigating?" he asked me.

"Probably not. So, what do you say? Are you game?"

"I'd love to," he said, though he did it with a frown.

"But," I supplied.

"But I promised your mother I was retired," he admitted. "Before you ask, that means informal amateur sleuthing as well. I wish I could help you, I really do, but without her blessing, I'm going to have to say no."

"I understand completely," I told him as I stood and reached for my jacket.

"Aren't you going to call and at least *ask* her?" he questioned me, practically pleading for me to do just that.

"Sorry, but I've learned to choose my battles with my mother over the years, and this is *not* one I care to fight, no offense intended."

"None taken," Phillip said, sighing a bit as he did. "Honestly, I don't blame you one bit. I've argued with her until I'm blue in the face, but the only crimes she's willing to let me investigate are ones I can do from halls of records and dusty old libraries." The retired police chief pointed to his desk, which was overflowing with papers, clippings, and copies. "It limits what I can do in the here and now, but at least it's something."

"I get it, Phillip. She doesn't want to risk losing both of us at the same time if things should go sideways."

He started to say something, paused, and then finally said, "I never thought of it that way, Suzanne."

"I didn't either until half an hour ago. I'd better be going."

"You're going to get *someone* to back you up though, right?" Phillip asked, the concern for my well-being clear in his voice.

"I promise," I said as I kissed his cheek. "Thanks for worrying about me."

"It turned into part of the job when I became your stepfather," he said. "Do me one last favor, would you?"

"If it doesn't involve calling my mother and pleading your case, you've got it," I answered.

"Take those with you," he said as he pointed to the sampled box of donuts.

"What am I supposed to do with them?" I asked him.

"Once they are out of here, I don't care. I just can't be trusted around them right now."

"I get that," I said as I retrieved the partially eaten box. "Happy hunting," I answered as I pointed to the piles of paper on his desk.

"Same to you," he replied, more than a bit forlorn that he wouldn't be joining me in my search for Samantha Peterson's killer.

After throwing the box of partially sampled treats in a bin near the curb, I got back into my Jeep and headed back toward town.

I had to find *someone* to help me investigate, but at that point, I had no idea who I should approach next.

My stomach growled a bit, so I decided to go by the Boxcar Grill to get a bite to eat. I never worked well on an empty stomach. My thoughts seemed to keep going back to my next meal instead of whatever it was I was working on. I had four dozen donuts in the back of my

Jeep, but frankly, I couldn't face the prospect of eating another one of my treats. I needed some good, solid comfort food, and since Momma's kitchen wasn't open at the moment, and I certainly didn't feel like making anything myself, Trish's diner was the next best thing.

It was slower than it should have been inside once I got there. Normally, at that time of day, I'd have to struggle to find a seat, but a good half of the diner's seating was empty.

"Wow, I didn't think you ever had lulls," I told Trish Granger as I approached her at the register.

"There's a new food cart parked on the edge of town that folks are trying out," she said. "They've stolen a good half of my business."

"I'm so sorry. What are you going to do about it?"

"Enjoy the lull," she said with a shrug. "Fads come and go. My regulars will come back soon enough, and in the meantime, it gives us all some time to catch our breaths."

"I haven't heard about the truck. What do they serve?"

"They claim to have a hundred different hot dog meals," she said.

"That sounds like a pretty limited menu," I answered.

"You'd be surprised. Besides the usual offerings of hot dogs with toppings, they've got corn dogs, hot dog soup, hot dog pizza, hot dog tacos, pigs in the blanket, hot dog omelets, hot dog casserole, and for all I know, hot dog ice cream."

"Still, nothing beats your comfort food," I told her.

"Suzanne, you don't have to buoy my spirits. Table for one?" she asked as she handed me a menu.

I refused it. "I'll take the special and a sweet tea."

"It's meatloaf, mashed potatoes, and green beans with a side of cornbread. Is that okay?"

"It sounds perfect," I told her.

"It does sound pretty good at that. Do you mind if I join you?"

"Not at all. I'd love the company," I answered.

"Is it okay if we sit up here by the register, just in case?" Trish asked me, her perennial ponytail bobbing as she spoke.

"That sounds good."

"Excellent. Let me grab our food and drinks, and I'll be right back."

She was gone less than a minute and soon returned with a tray filled with goodies. "Hilda's trying a new orange-pineapple cake. I grabbed us a couple of pieces, strictly as a taste test," she added with a grin.

"It will be a sacrifice, but I'll have dessert with you, if it's really that important to you." My smile was bigger than hers had been.

"I didn't think you'd mind," she answered as she served us. "I can't believe somebody whacked Samantha Peterson," Trish said after she finished her first bite of meatloaf. "I was the last person to see her alive, you know."

"I don't think so," I answered after a sip of sweet tea.

"Why, did someone *else* claim to?" she asked me.

"Well, for one, the killer saw her last," I corrected her.

"That's true enough. Still, I felt bad about the way our conversation ended. I'm afraid it's going to haunt me for a while."

"We weren't exactly best friends either," I told Trish, a little concerned about the heavy expression she wore. "What happened with you two?"

"I'm afraid we got into a bit of an argument," Trish said. "She thought I'd phoned in my clue, and I disagreed."

"I heard you did some kind of menu match," I told her.

"I had some old menus I found in storage that I was going to recycle anyway, so I cut them in half and put half of the next clue on one page and the rest on the other. Hang on a second—I'll show you." She grabbed two parts of an old menu and handed them to me. I liked the way she'd split the clue so that it made no sense at all without the other portion.

"What's wrong with this? I like it," I said as I handed the two halves back to her.

"So did I," she admitted. "I kind of lost my cool and told her to stick with her goal of unseating the mayor and leave me alone, and she didn't take the suggestion very well."

"Were those the exact words you used?" I asked her as I pointed my fork at her.

"Well, I might have said it a bit more colorfully than that," Trish acknowledged. "I regretted it the second I said it, but by the time I tried to catch up with her to apologize, she was gone, and now I'll never get the chance. I wish there was some way I could make it up to her."

"You just never know when your conversation with someone will be the last one you ever have, do you?" I asked her.

Trish shook her head, and then she took another bite. She was just about finished with her meal when she asked, "You're going to investigate, aren't you?"

"I might dig into it a bit," I admitted.

"Grace isn't helping you; I know for a fact she's out of town. Is Jake going to work with you?"

"He's going to Raleigh to visit his sister and her kids," I said.

"Then surely Dot or Phillip will do it."

"Momma's too busy, and Phillip has his own reasons for saying no," I admitted.

"That's perfect," Trish said with a smile.

"I hardly think so," I told her with a frown.

"Don't you see? *I* can help you," Trish said. Before I could interject, she added, "Hear me out, Suzanne. You told me a long time ago that I would be able to help you on a case sometime, and now would be perfect. Not only do I feel as though I owe the victim something, but it's slow here."

"It might not be your usual rush, but you still have customers to help," I told her. Honestly, I'd been thinking about approaching Paige Hill, the owner of our local bookstore and a natural-born sleuth if ever there was one.

"Hilda's been after me to take some time off so she can see what it's like to run the front. Gladys can handle the cooking, so it all lines up perfectly. What do you say?"

I could see from the earnest look in her gaze that she was serious. How could I say no to one of my best friends? Then again, I knew that Trish was even less interested in following rules than Grace was, and she would most likely be a handful. "Maybe."

"Why not? You need me, and I need to do this," Trish insisted.

"If you investigate with me, you have to do it my way, Trish," I told her. "That means following our agreed plan of attack."

"I can do that," she said solemnly.

"Can you really though? I've known you most of my life, and you aren't exactly a follower," I said. It may have been a little harsh, but better to hurt her feelings now than endanger her life later.

"Give me a chance. You'll see."

I didn't exactly have many other options, and I did love Trish dearly. I offered my hand, and as she shook it, I said, "You need to remember something. This isn't a game. Someone has been murdered, and we're going after the killer. It could get dangerous, and I mean deadly. You know how close I've come to ending up as a statistic myself, and I've been in the hospital more than once because of one of my investigations, not to mention the fact that I almost got our mayor killed helping me." George's busted leg from a killer trying to finish him off was a constant reminder to me that I wasn't just putting my own life in jeopardy. He didn't limp nearly as much as he used to, but when the weather was cold and rainy, I could still see the hitch in his stride. It was just as sobering now as it had been when he'd been struck down by that killer's car.

"I know that, Suzanne. I can do it. Trust me."

"I'm going to have to, with my life," I told her.

"You won't regret it," Trish said as she stood and started clearing away our dirty dishes, including the cake.

"Hey, I didn't get a chance to sample that dessert yet," I protested.

"I just figured you'd be in a hurry to get started."

"Trish, have you *ever* known me to be too busy for dessert?" I asked with a slight smile, trying to ease the solemn mood I'd created.

"That's fair," she said. "You eat yours, and I'll go talk to the ladies."

"Is Gladys here too?" I asked.

"Hilda called her in for the cake tasting. For the record, they both love it, but it still has to pass our approval."

"Then let's do our duty. It's only right," I added as I took a bite.

It was amazing.

"What do you think?"

I pretended to ponder the question for a moment. "I need to collect a bit more data before I'm ready to give my official opinion."

She wasn't fooled at all, which didn't surprise me. After Trish took a bite herself, she grinned. "Man, that's delightful. It's going on the weekend menu unless you have any objections."

"I can't say that I do, but I'm curious about something."

"Why the weekend only?" Trish asked.

"You've got it."

"I usually don't have any trouble keeping the place busy on weekdays, all current evidence to the contrary. If I offer special goodies only on the weekends, I tend to drive more traffic into the diner then."

"I like it, but I've got one suggestion."

"Hey, I'm always open to another opinion," she said. "Shoot."

"Sell it for a month during the week on a temporary basis that you announce from the start. Once your regulars get hooked on it, then move it to the weekends. They'll get hooked and have to come in just for that."

Trish grinned. "Wow, you don't *look* that devious."

"What can I say? Everybody's got a little bit of the devil in them."

"Some more than most," she replied. "Finish your cake. I'll be back in two minutes."

"I'll be here."

She started to collect her own partially finished cake plate when I reached for it and retrieved it from the tray.

"More research?" Trish asked with a slight smile.

"A girl can't be too thorough," I answered.

While Trish was in the Boxcar kitchen, sharing her plan with Hilda and Gladys, I saw one of my least favorite residents of April Springs come in, but I had to be cordial to him, since his daughter and wife both worked for me. Ray Blake was clearly looking for someone to interview about Samantha Peterson's murder, and it was obvious from the way he headed toward me that I was the one in his sights at the moment.

Chapter 5

"NO COMMENT," I SAID the moment Ray approached my table.

The newspaperman frowned. "I haven't even asked you anything yet, Suzanne."

"Think of it as a preemptive strike, Ray," I answered.

"I just wanted to give you a chance to comment on something I heard regarding you and Donut Hearts before I go to print," he said, inviting himself to sit in the chair Trish had just vacated.

"I have an attorney on retainer. Be careful about what you threaten," I told him icily. That wasn't exactly true, but Momma had an attorney, and I knew if I asked, she'd have him represent me. Still, I wasn't about to say that my mother would do something if he was mean to me. It was just a bit too childish to say, even if I could manage to couch it in an adult conversation.

"Take it easy, Suzanne," Ray said, clearly trying to defuse the situation. "Your donut shop is very dear to my wife and daughter. I'm trying to protect their interests here, too."

"And if you happen to sell a few newspapers along the way, that's okay too, right? What are you looking for here, Ray? Cover from any fallout your story might create?"

I could see that I'd scored a direct hit with my comment. "Like I said before, I'm just trying to be fair," he stammered. I had him, and we both knew it.

"Really? Fair? You?"

"You don't have to sound so incredulous," he answered.

Was he actually hurt by my remark? I highly doubted it, but there was a slight twinge that told me maybe I'd gone too far. I might not have liked the man, but that didn't mean I wanted to completely alienate him, either.

"What do you want me to comment on?" I asked him, trying to keep my tone calm and even.

"Is it true that one of your donut-making tools was used as a murder weapon?"

"No," I stated flatly. "Next question."

"No?" he asked, clearly in disbelief. "I have it from a very good source that it was one of your donut cutters that was used in the crime."

"Get your facts straight, Ray. It was a paperweight." It suddenly occurred to me that I'd done what I'd warned Emma not to; I'd fed her father a fact about the case. As he started to take notes, I said, "That is off the record."

"For that to work, you have to tell me that *before* you answer my questions," he replied smugly.

"Okay. You know it was a paperweight. What you don't know is what kind of paperweight it was and how it tied in to Donut Hearts." It was my only way out, enticing him with more information than I'd already given him. It was a gamble but one that I had to take.

"I'm listening."

"If you let me tell you, you can't print *anything* I say, including the fact that I told you it was a paperweight," I said.

"No deal," he said as he stood.

"Fine," I replied as I pulled out my cell phone.

"Who are you calling? You should know that your husband doesn't scare me, and you can't use my wife and daughter against me either. We've come to an agreement that my reporting is beyond their control. As long as I print the truth, they're fine with it."

"I wasn't calling *any* of them," I said, which wasn't true at all. I'd had Emma's number ready to dial when he told me it was no longer a threat, so I decided to go with my last and most deadly option.

"Then who are you going to call?"

"My mother," I said.

His face went three shades of pale. "Hold on a second. There's no reason to be rash."

"Why? Have you suddenly had a change of heart?" I asked a bit maliciously. Anyone with any sense at all knew that when my mother was defending me, she was as fierce as a grizzly protecting her cubs.

"You've got a deal," Ray said.

"What deal in particular are you willing to make?"

"You give me more information, and I won't print *any* of it unless I get outside confirmation."

"That wasn't part of our agreement," I reminded him.

"Maybe not, but it's the only one you're going to get. Take it or leave it."

"I'll take it," I said. I knew when he was digging in his heels and when I could push him a bit harder, and he was clearly resolute about his position.

"The murder weapon was a cast iron donut that could be used as a paperweight, but I had it as a display piece. It is the size of a regular donut, hollow on the inside but still pretty hefty, with strawberry icing painted on the top and raised sprinkles."

"How much does it weigh?"

"I'd have to guess not much more than a pound," I said.

He looked at me sharply. "How could something that weighs that little be used as a murder weapon?"

"You'll have to ask the police that," I told him, "but a pound applied to the right place is clearly more than enough to kill."

"Was it the only one of its kind?" he asked me. I had to give Ray credit. He was certainly being thorough.

"It was from a set of three: one chocolate, one vanilla, and one strawberry."

"Could it be cherry?" he asked.

"I suppose it's possible, but I've always thought of it as strawberry. What could that possibly matter, Ray?"

"You never know what's going to matter," he answered, which I knew was true enough. "Where exactly was she struck?"

"Asked and answered, Ray. Talk to the chief." I wasn't about to let him trap me into giving him even more information than I already had. "I've been very cooperative and given you more than I should have. Do you have anything you can tell me?"

"Are you investigating the murder yourself, Suzanne?" He paused a moment before answering his own question. "Of course you are. Something of yours was used as a murder weapon."

"I may be curious about it," I admitted.

"Come on. It's more than that, and we both know it." He was getting a bit smug again, but there was really nothing I could do about it.

"What have you found out so far, Ray?"

The newspaper publisher looked around to see if anyone was listening to our conversation, but fortunately, no one was close enough to follow along. "I understand Samantha was about to fire her assistant, Gray, after the scavenger hunt. *He* certainly had reason to kill her."

"Why was she going to fire him?" I asked. The man had been a bit mousy for my taste, and I had a difficult time imagining him swinging my cast iron donut with so much force that it would kill his boss, but then again, I knew from experience that people could do the most unimaginable things when their backs were up against the wall.

"That's confidential," Ray said.

"Meaning you don't know," I retorted.

"Meaning I'm not going to tell you," he answered.

"I'll just have to find out myself, then," I told him as Trish walked up to the table.

"Am I interrupting anything?" she asked.

"As a matter of fact, Ray was just leaving," I answered before the newspaperman could comment.

"We're not finished here, Suzanne," he said, refusing to get up.

"I'm sorry, but you're mistaken. We are," I told him.

"You heard the lady," Trish said as she used her knee to nudge the chair he was sitting on. The physical act was enough to catch him off guard, and Ray nearly tumbled out of his chair. "Move on, Sport."

"But I want lunch," he protested.

"Sorry, we're all out. Now go."

She stood there, staring at Ray, until he had no choice but to stand and leave. As he was going, I called out, "Remember our agreement, Ray."

"I won't forget. Any of this," he added as he stared at Trish a moment longer than he should have before walking out the door.

"You didn't have to kick him out on my account," I told her after he was gone.

"I don't like the man bothering my diners," she said.

"Still," I prodded.

"Don't worry about Ray. He'll be back for lunch tomorrow, and neither one of us will act as though any of this happened. Great news! Hilda and Gladys are as excited as I am about our plan for the next few days. They're going to run the Boxcar, and I'm going to catch a killer."

Trish looked a little too gleeful as she said it.

"Remember, we're going to be on the outskirts of the case, asking questions and gathering information. Don't expect a dramatic conclusion or even a guarantee that we'll figure out who killed Samantha Peterson."

"Don't undersell our abilities, Suzanne. With your brains and my bravado, how can we fail? Now let's go. We've got suspects to grill, clues to uncover, and confessions to extort."

What had I gotten myself into? It seemed that I was going to have more than enough on my hands trying to keep Trish in check, let alone trying to solve a murder.

As I raced out the door after her, I wondered where she was going in such a hurry, since we hadn't even discussed our next move.

"Hang on a second," I said once I caught her at the bottom of the steps of the Boxcar Grill.

"What's the matter, can't keep up?" she asked me with a smile.

"I'm just wondering where you're going with such confidence," I answered.

"I figured we'd head over to the hospital and examine the body for clues," Trish said confidently.

"This isn't a TV show or even a book, Trish. We can't just waltz into the morgue and start poking around."

"It'll be okay. I know a guy who works there. He'll let us poke all we want to."

I pulled her to one side. "The problem is that we don't even know what to look for, even if it was okay for us to inspect Samantha's body, which it most certainly is not."

"Then what are we supposed to do?" Trish asked me.

"I'd like to check out the gazebo," I admitted as I pointed over to it. It was within fifty feet of us, and even from there, I could see the yellow crime scene tape fluttering in the breeze.

"What makes you think there's anything there to see?"

"I don't know. I suppose I just want to get a feel for what happened," I admitted.

"Fine. Let's go. I've got a pocketknife, so I'll cut the police tape so we can get a closer look."

I put a hand on her shoulder. "Nobody's cutting any tape, Trish. We're going to walk around the edges, but we aren't going to cross the line." I'd meant it in more than the literal way, but I had a feeling that the implication was going to be lost on Trish.

"Okay, fine. We'll do it your way," she replied, clearly looking a bit disappointed that I wasn't willing to break the police barrier, no matter how flimsy it might be.

As we approached the gazebo, I saw the area staked out where the body was most likely found.

"Where's the chalk outline?" Trish asked as she studied the rough ground.

"They don't do that," I answered.

"There's no tape or anything? Why not?"

"They don't want to disturb any evidence there might be," I replied.

There were some red flags on thin wires that marked the general location, but all in all, it wasn't nearly as impressive as they made it look on television, not that they could use chalk on the dirt and fallen leaves, anyway. It was February after all, and while most of the leaves had been collected and hauled away, there were still quite a few errant piles scattered around the park. The gazebo itself was taped off, as well as a perimeter of trees near where the body must have been discovered. The brush was thick around that part of the park, and as I headed for the general vicinity of the taped-off area, I saw movement through the brush. Without a word, I started running toward whoever was hiding there. I was hoping I'd see who it was before they even knew I was after them, but that was soon foiled by my helper.

"Where's the fire, Suzanne? Why are you running?" Trish called out as she started after me.

Whoever had been lurking had to have heard her, because the next thing I knew, whoever it had been had bolted for the road.

I followed, but before I could get a glimpse of who it might have been, they had broken through the brush and had vanished.

Chapter 6

"WHO ARE WE CHASING?" Trish asked as she caught up with me.

"I don't know," I admitted as I tried to catch my breath. I wasn't exactly fit, at least not in good enough shape to chase people through the park. Then again, I made donuts for a living, which wasn't exactly a cardio workout every day.

"Then why were we chasing them?" she asked, clearly puzzled.

"Someone was watching us," I told her. "I wanted to see who it was."

"Geez, Suzanne, that sounds like you're being a little paranoid to me."

I turned to face her. "Trish, this isn't working out. I'm sorry."

She looked shocked and not just a little hurt. "You're *firing* me? Seriously? I was just joking."

"That's the thing. You think this is just fun and games, and you're not nearly scared enough for this to work. Being paranoid when I'm working on solving a case has been the *only* thing that has kept me alive more than once. If you're *not* paranoid, then you're going to take foolish risks, and where murder is involved, you don't get any second chances."

I had started to walk away when Trish reached out and grabbed my arm. "Hey, I'm sorry. Okay? Give me a chance."

"I did," I said, perhaps a bit harsher than I should have, but I wasn't about to risk both of our lives because she wasn't taking the dangers more seriously.

"Come on, Suzanne. You know what I mean. Please?"

I hadn't heard that much contrition in her voice the entire time I'd known her. "Do you *really* want to do this, or is it just something that sounds like fun to you?" I asked, staring into her eyes and holding her gaze.

"I spoke with that woman, had an argument in fact, and less than half an hour later, she was dead," Trish said in a serious tone. "I know

I come off all confident and brash, but that shook me to the core. You never know how much time you have left, and the fact that someone killed her really shook me up. I can't imagine how I'm going to go to sleep tonight if I don't do something to make things right. Let me help you figure out what happened to her."

She was sincere; there was no doubt about that in my mind. Maybe I'd been a bit too harsh with her after all. "Will you promise to take this seriously from now on?" I asked.

"I promise," she replied, and I believed her.

"Fine," I said, but before she could get too excited, I added, "But remember, you're on probation, Trish. If I catch you taking this lightly one more time, you're off the case. Are you willing to live with that condition, or should we call it quits now?"

"I can do it," she said solemnly.

"Okay then," I answered as I headed back to the brush. "Let's give it another shot."

"Are we going after whoever was watching us?" she asked me softly.

"Whoever it was is long gone by now," I replied, "but maybe we'll get lucky and they left a clue behind."

As I headed into the brush where the lurker had been, Trish asked, "Am I allowed to ask you questions?"

Wow, I must have been harsher than I'd realized. "Of course you can."

"How can we be sure whoever was watching us is involved in the case?"

"We can't," I answered, "but we have to assume that everything that happens from here on out is connected to Samantha's murder until we prove it otherwise. That includes any clues we find that might turn out to be red herrings or suspects we have that end up being innocent."

"If I've learned anything in my life, it's that no one is truly innocent," she said.

"I mean of murder," I corrected myself.

"Fair enough."

As we poked through the brush, Trish called out, "There's a candy bar wrapper over here."

She was so excited I hated to burst her bubble when I joined her. "Good work, but that's not a clue."

"How can you be so sure?" she asked.

"Look at the edges of the wrapper," I said. "It's starting to fade from the elements. This has been out in the weather for at least a few weeks, unless I miss my guess."

She leaned down and studied the wrapper a little more closely. "I missed that."

"It happens," I told her.

"You didn't," she insisted.

"I've been doing this awhile," I admitted. "Keep looking."

We pushed on, but there was nothing out of the ordinary, no shoe prints, no discarded trash, nothing that looked as though it might be a clue as to the identity of the lurker.

Trish looked disappointed when I said, "Let's go back and look at where the body was discovered."

"I was sure we'd find something," she said.

"Most of the things we check out are going to be dead ends," I told her. "Don't let it discourage you. Finding something that leads us in the right direction is worth every blind alley we go down along the way."

"I've got to admit that this isn't quite what I thought it would be," she said as we moved toward where the body had been discovered by Dr. Hicks.

"The truth is that it's a lot of dull grunt work that sometimes culminates in a few moments of abject terror, and that's just if you're lucky," I told her with a shrug.

"And you actually *like* doing this?" she asked me gently.

"The investigative work is fine, but I do what I do for the victims who can't do it for themselves anymore," I admitted.

"So, you're like Batman," she said without a hint of irony in her voice.

"Trust me, I am *nothing* like Batman," I said with a smile.

"Maybe a little," Trish insisted.

"Not one little bit," I told her.

"Fine, you're not Batman," Trish replied. "Superman?"

I had to laugh. "I'm just a donut maker who wants to see the world make sense, where people get punished for the bad things they do," I answered.

"So then, maybe a little like Batman after all," she said softly.

I wasn't sure I was supposed to hear it, so I decided to ignore her comment and press on. I had a smile on my lips, but it quickly disappeared when I got to where the body had been found.

That took all of the humor right out of me, knowing that not that long ago, a woman had lost her life there.

It was time again for the serious business of tracking down her killer.

"Where to now?" Trish asked as we headed for my Jeep after we'd looked at the crime scene itself.

"I'd like to talk to Gray Blackhurst," I told her.

"Samantha's assistant? Why?"

"While you were in the kitchen at the Boxcar, Ray Blake told me that Samantha was getting ready to fire him. Knowing Ray, it's probably not true, but Gray is still the best person to start with."

"Why was she going to fire him?" Trish asked as we got in and buckled up. We could have easily walked to city hall from the gazebo, but I wasn't sure where our next clue might lead us, and I wanted to have transportation close by. There was no question of us taking Trish's car. It was constantly breaking down around town, and I didn't want to put my trust in it to get us to city hall, let alone Union Square if we needed to go there later.

"Ray didn't say, which means that he didn't know. Let's go ask Gray."

We pulled into the visitor's parking area of city hall and walked into the building. It was easy enough finding Samantha Peterson's office. It was the door covered in flowers and cards. How had the town mobilized so quickly in creating a memorial for the woman? She hadn't been all that beloved as far as I knew, and besides, it had been hours, not days, since she'd been murdered. Still, Samantha had been one of our own, and the folks of April Springs tended to take that personally, none more than I did.

Gray's office, a cubby the size of a modest closet, was dark as we approached.

There was a redhead at the main reception desk who was new, at least to me. She noticed what we were doing and approached us. Stylish, thin, and pretty in a dainty sort of way, she was probably in her late twenties or early thirties, and she had the most striking blue eyes and pale skin I'd ever seen. "Are you looking for Gray too?" she asked us in a soft voice.

"Too?" I asked her.

"A reporter was here earlier, and so was the police chief," she said.

Trish stepped forward and offered her hand. "I don't believe we've met. I'm Trish Granger. I own the Boxcar Grill, and this is Suzanne Hart."

"Of Donut Hearts fame?" she asked me with a smile.

"One and the same. Are you a fan?"

"I am," she said with a frown, which still somehow managed to be adorable. "They are my weakness in life."

"Funny, but I don't remember you coming in," I told her. Surely I would have recalled so striking a young woman in my shop.

"That's because I don't trust myself around your treats," she answered. "I'm Hannahlee Cumbersome."

"Any relation to old Doc Cumbersome?" I asked. He'd been the town doctor when I was a kid, long before my stepfather, Phillip, had been the police chief.

"He was my grandfather," she said with a gentle smile. "Did you know him well?"

"He brought me a banana split when I was in the hospital with a broken leg," I said, remembering the kindly old man fondly.

"That sounds like something he would do. I decided to move back here after my mother passed away."

"Was she from here too?" I asked, naturally curious, or just plain nosy, however folks liked to look at it.

"No, she and Grandpa had a falling out when she was a kid, and she left here to live with my grandmother." She seemed to realize how much information she was giving us. "Listen to me natter on. I usually don't share my family history with everyone I meet."

"Folks say I'm a good listener," I told her. "Welcome to April Springs, Hannahlee."

"Thanks," she said.

"Do you have any idea where we might find Gray?" Trish asked. Funny, she was doing the investigating I should have been doing myself.

"All I can tell you is what I told everyone else. He hasn't been back since poor Ms. Peterson was murdered."

"He disappeared?" Trish asked.

Hannahlee looked troubled by that choice of words. "It's not like he vanished or anything. He's probably off somewhere, grieving."

"Were they close?" I asked her as sympathetically as I could muster.

"Not that I was able to tell," she said. "That's not a particularly kind thing to say, is it? Please forget I said anything."

"Have you seen anything that made you say that?" Trish pressed her.

I could see Hannahlee's back stiffen. I tried to smooth things over with her. "We're not being nosy. Samantha was killed with something of mine that I treasured, a cast iron donut. We're just trying to make sense of it all, you know?"

Hannahlee responded to that, and I could see her posture ease a bit. "I understand. How terrible that must be for you."

"It was even worse for Samantha," Trish butted in. "Talk to us, Hannahlee."

At that moment, I heard a phone ringing at the desk she'd left to greet us. "If you'll excuse me, I need to get that."

After she was gone, I turned to Trish. "That wasn't a very subtle way to question someone who is under no obligation to talk to us."

"Wow, don't hold back, Suzanne. Tell me how you really feel."

"You could have just cost us a valuable piece of information with your approach. It's unacceptable, Trish."

She looked at me aghast. "What exactly did I do that was so wrong?"

"You made a demand instead of a request," I told her. "We can't force anyone to talk to us. That means we need to use skill, subtlety, and finesse. Do you understand?"

"I get it. It's just that you were taking so long getting her family history that I thought we needed to speed things along."

"I wanted to get to know her a bit as a person before I started grilling her, Trish. Besides, she's a new resident of April Springs. I wanted to know more about her. This isn't just about a murder case, you know. It's about connecting with people on a personal basis."

"So you were just *pretending* to be interested to get her to talk to us?" Trish asked.

"No!" I said a little more forcefully than I probably should have. I noticed that a few folks glanced our way, including Hannahlee, who was still on the phone or at least pretending to be until we left. Bringing my voice back down, I added, "I *am* interested in her. I've seen you stop and talk to diners for no reason other than you want to be welcoming, and don't bother trying to deny it."

"Sure, but that's different."

"In what way?" I asked her, sincerely interested in her answer.

"I wasn't investigating a murder when that happened," she said.

"You need to treat this differently. We don't have any authority or even permission to investigate this crime. We find folks, ask questions, and listen. Sometimes, we dig up a clue or two along the way, but this is an interpersonal experience, not some kind of treasure hunt for a killer."

"Sorry," she said. "I guess I kind of got wrapped up in solving this thing."

"In a few hours?" I asked her. "It usually takes days, weeks, even months to figure out who the guilty party is. Phillip is working on a case right now that goes back decades. There aren't any quick solutions, at least not usually. Patience is critical, and so is paying attention. Momma always told me growing up that you don't learn anything by talking, only by listening. I try to ask the right questions and then sit back and let folks talk. You'd be amazed what you can pick up doing that."

"Is that your secret? Listening?" She seemed incredulous that it was even possible.

"It's a big part of it. Did you hear Hannahlee earlier? She said she told us more than she'd planned to, but I'm known as a good listener. It's something I've cultivated over the years. Not enough folks know how to ask a question and listen to the answer instead of thinking about the next thing they're going to say."

"Lesson learned," Trish said. "I'll try to do better."

"You'll be okay," I replied.

"Do you really think so?" There was more than a touch of hopefulness in her gaze.

"I'd like to think so," I answered. "Now, the next person we speak with, try something for me."

"What's that?"

"Just listen," I answered.

"That's really it?"

"It's harder than it sounds. Trust me," I told her when my cell phone rang.

I was about to ignore it when I saw who was calling, and it was someone I never put off if there was any way around it.

"Jake, how's the drive going?"

"I just passed Statesville," he said. "Sorry I didn't hang around. How did the scavenger hunt go?"

"You haven't heard, have you?"

"Heard what?" my husband asked me.

"Someone killed Samantha Peterson with one of my cast iron donuts."

"Suzanne, that's terrible," he answered after a moment. "How exactly did they manage that? Those things barely weigh a pound."

"I'm guessing she was struck in the temple with one," I said softly, staring at the nearby memorial for the woman in question. It felt a little creepy talking about her murder with everything so close.

"Want me to come back?"

"I appreciate that, but your sister needs you," I told him.

"Not as much as you do. Grace is out of town. Does that mean you have your mother or at least Phillip helping you work on the case?"

"What makes you think I'm doing any such thing?" I asked him.

"Because I know you? Who's helping you?"

"Trish Granger," I answered.

He chuckled for a moment before speaking again. "Seriously, who is working on the case with you? You're not doing it alone, are you?"

I didn't know how to respond to that, so I handed Trish my phone. "My husband wants to say hello."

She took the phone from me. "Hi, Jake. How are tricks? Sure. Yes. Okay. Here she is." She handed it back to me as she said, "He wants to talk to you." Trish looked puzzled by something, no doubt Jake's reaction to her being involved in my investigation.

When I got back on the line, my husband asked, "Suzanne, is that really such a good idea? Trish is a bit forceful, don't you think?"

"It's going to be fine," I said. I wanted to tell him that she wasn't my first choice or even my fourth, but I didn't know how to do it without shaking Trish's confidence or hurting her feelings.

"You can't tell me the real reason, can you? What happened, was everyone else busy?"

"Something like that," I said. "Let me know when you get to Sarah's place, okay?"

"I will. Suzanne, don't forget that she's a rookie at this. You're going to have to watch *both* your backs."

"I don't think it's going to snow, but you never know," I answered.

"Fine. Just be careful."

"You, too."

Once he hung up, Trish smiled at me. "I take it Jake was surprised by your choice of investigating partners?"

"What makes you say that?"

"Come on, don't kid a kidder."

I decided to tell her the truth. "He was a little concerned about our safety, since you've never done this before."

"You had to start somewhere too, right?"

I thought back to the first body I'd ever found and then meeting Jake soon after. In a way, it seemed like yesterday, but in another, it had been a lifetime ago. "I did. It hasn't been easy."

"I don't expect it to be, but I won't let you down."

When she didn't say anything else, I answered, "I trust you."

Trish nodded. "Since we can't find Gray, who is next on our list?"

"I'd like to speak with Doctor Hicks," I admitted. "I wonder if she's at the hospital."

"There's one way to find out," Trish said.

"By going there?"

"That's what I was thinking."

"Then let's go."

I turned to look at Hannahlee, and I offered her a small wave and a smile as I headed for the door. She waved back rather tentatively, and I wondered what had really brought her to April Springs. It wasn't that I thought she had lied to me, it was just that I suspected there was more to the story than she'd shared with us. One of these days, I was going to ask her again, and with any luck, she'd find that I was someone who would be happy to listen to her.

I probably wouldn't bring Trish along though.

After all, she was new to the listening game, and I was a seasoned old pro. I had faith that Trish could learn the skills she needed to be an asset to my investigation, but I still wasn't sure she had the temperament. Time would tell, but I wouldn't truly know until we were faced with a dire situation where our lives were threatened. Only then would I get to see if she had the right stuff.

I just hoped that it wouldn't be too late to see that sleuthing wasn't in her wheelhouse if she buckled under the pressure.

If it was, then it might be the last chance either one of us ever had.

Chapter 7

WE CAUGHT A BREAK AS we drove into the hospital parking lot. Dr. Hicks was just getting into her flashy sports car, and I flagged her down.

"What's wrong, Suzanne? Is someone hurt?" she asked me when she saw that I'd rushed to her parking spot.

"We just need a minute of your time," I told her.

Zoey looked at her watch and frowned. "That's about all I have. I need to get over to Maple Hollow pronto."

"Is it some kind of medical emergency?" Trish asked her.

Dr. Hicks shrugged her shoulders, lifting her short dress even higher than it already was. I had heard that Zoey Hicks was a good doctor, but it was hard to remember sometimes when I saw the way she dressed. I suppose if I had a body like hers, I'd be more willing to show it off, but then again, probably not. I had never gone in for flash, something my husband claimed to love about me, but I knew a great many men responded to the way Zoey Hicks presented herself to the world.

"What can I do for you ladies?"

"We're curious about how you found Samantha Peterson," I said.

"Deceased," she said simply.

"Care to give us any more details than that?" I asked her as politely as I could.

"Why on earth would you want to know?" she asked.

It was a fair question. "The woman was murdered using one of my valuables that was stolen today from the donut shop. How could I not be curious about what happened?"

Zoey paused a moment, clearly in thought. "Fine. One blow to the left temple was all it took. I wager she died fairly quickly. That cast iron donut must have hit the exact right spot, or in her case, the exact wrong one. Do you want a detailed medical description of what killed her, or are layman's terms good enough for you?"

"Doctor, did I say something to upset you?" I asked her softly.

"Why do you ask?"

"You seem a bit tense," I answered.

"And terse, too," Trish added, which wasn't necessary, though it was indeed true.

Zoey Hicks frowned for a moment before speaking. "I deal with death in my profession as a matter of course, and since I became the coroner for the area, I've seen more than my fair share of it, but stumbling across a murder victim myself was a new one on me."

"I know just how that feels," I told her sympathetically.

"Yes, you do, don't you?" she asked. "It's startling, isn't it?"

"To say the least," I replied.

Trish at least had the sense not to add anything to the conversation.

"What do you want to know?" the doctor asked gently.

"Where was Luke while you were finding the body?" Trish asked, ruining the mood.

"He went to get us coffee," she said, snapping a bit at her.

"Where? We know for a fact that he didn't come by the Boxcar Grill, and he certainly didn't go back to Donut Hearts," Trish pushed.

"How should *I* know where he went? Ask him," she said.

"You don't know? What does *he* think about what happened?" I asked gently, trying to get some insight into their dynamic.

"I don't know, and frankly, I don't care. The truth is that I don't think I'll be seeing him anymore," she said.

"Because of what happened to Samantha?" Trish asked.

"The reasons are no concern of yours," the doctor said brusquely. "Now I really must go. Your minute was up two minutes ago."

I tried to delay her, but she wouldn't allow it.

After she drove off, Trish said, "I know. You don't have to say it. I need to listen more and talk less. I can't believe how hard it is to do."

"Try harder," I told her.

"Ouch. True, but painful. I will. Do you believe her?" Trish asked, only partially put off by my admonition.

"Which part?"

"Any of it," Trish said. "I don't believe *she* broke up with *him*, for starters."

"Why not?"

"She definitely had a 'woman scorned' vibe to me," she explained. "And how about the lame story of him going for coffee?"

"I thought it was believable," I said. "It has been awfully chilly today."

"True, but let's assume they were walking from the Boxcar to the gazebo. All Luke had to do was turn around and come back to the diner, and if he didn't want to do that, you're the next closest place that sells hot beverages. Where was he going, to the grocery store to get some of the swill they sell there? I don't think so."

"That all makes sense, but if he wasn't going for coffee, then where was he?"

"That's something we need to ask him, don't you think?" Trish asked me.

"I suppose that should be our next stop," I replied as I got back into the Jeep and headed back into town.

We found Luke out in front of his house, taking down his Christmas lights. Most folks around town took theirs down in January, but evidently, Luke was a lingerer. That was nothing, though. A few folks left their lights up all year round, turning them on during the Fourth of July as well as Christmas and every other holiday besides.

At least we had a captive audience. Luke was up on a ladder, twenty feet in the air, pulling down lights, so he couldn't exactly run away from us.

"Do you have a minute, Luke?" I asked him as we approached the ladder.

He nearly lost his balance and had to steady himself against the gutter to keep from falling. "Geez, Suzanne, don't sneak up on a man on a ladder."

"Sorry," I said as I helped steady it from the ground. "We'd like to talk about what happened this afternoon."

"I don't want to discuss it," he said as he kept yanking lights off of their clips and letting the string fall to the ground.

"We've already spoken to Zoey," Trish said. It was the exact right thing to say, and I found myself believing that maybe Trish was going to work out as an investigating partner after all.

Maybe.

"I can only imagine what she told you. Let me guess. She claimed that *she* broke up with *me*. Am I right?"

"That's not what happened?" I asked him, craning my neck upward. It was awkward reading his face from so far away, so I really couldn't tell how truthful he was being with me.

"*I* dumped *her*," he said flatly. "If it helps her bruised ego to tell folks otherwise, that's her business, not mine."

"But you two seemed so happy together at the donut shop this morning," I said, which was a complete and utter lie.

"Did you hear the same conversation I did? She kept trying to protect me from Samantha. I never needed her to do that, and I surely didn't ask her to. Those two women took an instant dislike to each other."

"Well, you went from one of them to the other fairly quickly," Trish said.

I thought that was a bit harsh, but for once, Trish's directness got a response that was helpful. "They had a problem with each other long before I came into the picture," he said. "The two of them have had a history of squabbles that goes way back."

"Still, it couldn't help that you dumped Samantha and went after Zoey immediately after winning the lottery," Trish said.

He jerked so hard as he whipped his head toward her that I thought he might fall. "I was an idiot, okay? I never should have gone out with Zoey Hicks in the first place."

"Does that mean you wish you had stayed with Samantha?" I asked him.

"No. We weren't right for each other, whether I was rich or poor, sick or healthy. She just couldn't get it through her head that Zoey wasn't the reason we broke up."

"What *was* the reason?" I asked, hoping to get some idea of what his motivation had been. Part of it was for the case, but some of it was out of curiosity, something I had no short supply of naturally.

"She tried to control my life, and then I managed to find myself a woman who was even worse about it. I'm through with dating, at least for a while."

"Why weren't you with Zoey when she found the body?" I asked.

"We broke up on the way to the gazebo. Why would I still be with her to win a romantic getaway I was never going to take? I don't think so."

"She said you were going for coffee," Trish pointed out.

"Coffee? Really? Is that what she said? Well, she's lying."

"At least one of you is," Trish said.

That was more than he was willing to take. Luke started down the ladder, and he wasn't a bit happy about it. "Are you calling me a liar?" he asked Trish as he descended.

"Take it easy, Luke," I said as I moved away to let him down. As I did, I stepped between the two of them, just in case Luke decided to get violent. I had never seen this side of the man before, and it was illuminating. I would never have suspected that he was capable of murder, but now I wasn't so sure. There was a fire in his eyes that scared me a bit.

"I won't stand here and take that kind of talk from anyone," he said, and then he pointed a finger at Trish. "Get off my property."

"I didn't mean anything by it," Trish said, trying to backpedal. She was clearly shaken by his sudden display of anger.

"I don't care. Go."

I grabbed Trish's arm and pulled her away. "Come on. Let's get out of here."

Once we were in the Jeep, I started to give Trish another lecture, but when I looked at her, I saw she was sporting a broad grin.

"What on earth are you smiling about?" I asked her.

"It worked, didn't it? I wanted to see if I could get a reaction out of him, but boy oh boy, I never expected that!"

"You're *happy* that he wanted to go for your throat?" I asked her incredulously.

"He doesn't scare me, Suzanne. I wanted to see if he was capable of hitting Samantha in the head with that deadly donut of yours. Is there any doubt in your mind that he could have done it?"

"No," I admitted, "but it was a risky thing to do."

"I'm not afraid of Luke Davenport," Trish said smugly.

"No? What if he is the killer? Do you think it would be that difficult for him to kill again? You can't put yourself in his crosshairs like that, Trish. It's just not safe."

"He wasn't going to do anything with you standing right there," she said, but the confidence in her voice was a little shaky.

"Maybe not, but I'm not always going to be there. Stop taking unnecessary chances, or we're finished investigating. You know what? Maybe we should call it a day. We gave it our best shot, but it didn't work out."

"Hang on, Suzanne. See it from my side. If I hadn't goaded him, would you have ever believed that mild-mannered Luke Davenport had that in him? Be honest."

"No," I admitted. "His reaction caught me off guard, too."

"So maybe there's something to my method after all," Trish said.

"Maybe, but it's not worth being killed over," I told her.

"That's fair. How about if I dial it back some, say half of the full Trish?" she asked me, clearly trying to charm her way out of it.

"One tenth, at the max," I said, not returning her smile. "Deal?"

"Deal."

"Trish, this is it. You aren't getting any more warnings. One more outburst like that, and I'm walking away from you, at least as far as this or any other murder investigation is concerned. Do I make myself clear?"

"Crystal," she said. "Where should we go next?"

"Well, we have at least three more people we need to speak with today," I said.

"Care to share your list with me?" she asked.

"Gunther Peale, Thompson Smythe, and George Morris," I said.

"The mayor? Really?"

"I don't like it any more than you do, probably even less, but it has to be done," I told her.

"Should we tackle him first?" Trish asked.

"I'm going to need some time to work up the nerve," I answered. "Let's find Gunther and Thompson first."

"Deal," she said.

As I drove toward Gunther Peale's place, I found myself again doubting whether Trish had been the right choice as an investigating partner. She was too rash, too blunt for the subtle approach I preferred, and while Grace could be a wild card at times, I wasn't completely sure I could trust Trish not to put both of our lives in jeopardy. Her goading of a murder suspect had rattled me, and I thought about walking away then and there.

But that might mean that Samantha Peterson's killer could go free, and I couldn't allow that.

I'd have to push on, but I promised myself that if Trish put either one of us in danger one more time, I was going to have to live with letting Chief Grant and his police force find the killer or fail.

Life was too valuable to throw away or even to risk unnecessarily.

Chapter 8

GUNTHER'S YARD WAS filled with stone walls, stone walkways, and a stone fountain that took up half the space he had. The retired mason was at work on a new addition, an outdoor fireplace made of, surprise surprise, stone.

"I haven't seen your yard since you retired. It's absolutely stunning," I said as I took it all in. Trish just nodded, and I hoped that was a new norm for her behavior in our investigation.

"What can I say?" Gunther asked with a grin. "I'm a man of limited interests."

"Don't sell yourself short," I told him. "This is pure artistry."

"It's getting to be a lost art, that's for sure," he said. As he flexed his large weathered and worn hands, he said, "I can't do this all day long anymore, but I nibble at it for an hour or two every day. It relaxes me."

"It *has* been a stressful day, hasn't it, given what happened to Samantha Peterson," I commented, watching him for a reaction.

"Nice segue. So, that's why you're here. The sleuth of April Springs is back at it, is she?"

"What makes you say that?" I asked him, doing my best to act confused by his apt description of my behavior.

"Come on, Suzanne. Trish is admittedly a new addition to the team, but I had a feeling you'd be nosing around in this case before the sun set today, and I was right. Thompson owes me ten bucks," he added with a bit of glee in his voice and a new twinkle in his eye.

"I hadn't realized you were even aware of what I've been doing," I told him.

"Nobody watches what they say in front of a stonemason, especially one who is as quiet as I am when I work. I've done jobs all around April Springs, Union Square, Maple Hollow, and half a dozen other towns in the area. Trust me, your reputation precedes you."

"I just hate to see murder go unpunished," I told him, glancing at Trish. She seemed quite amused by the situation, but at least for now, she was limiting her contribution to a grin that she didn't even try to squelch when she caught me looking at her.

"I couldn't agree with you more," he said. "So, from your presence here, I take it I made it onto your list of suspects. Good for you."

"What makes you assume that?"

"You're here, aren't you? Besides, Thompson and I had a pretty public brawl with the lady not an hour before someone up and killed her." He flexed his hands again, and I noticed a few fresh scratches on them. Gunther saw my glance and explained, "I had to retrieve a few spare blocks I've been keeping out back, and the wild roses scratched me up pretty good as I was getting them out. You'd think my hands would be tough as leather by now, and the palms and fingers are, but the backs of my hands are relatively unscathed." He kneaded one spot as he added, "At least they were."

"Since it's out in the open, would you mind telling us the last time you saw Samantha Peterson?" I asked him.

He paused a moment before answering. "That would be as I was storming off from the argument Thompson and I had with her in city hall. She was almost as angry with us as we were with her, but I can assure you that all three of us were very much alive when Thompson and I left."

"So, where did you go after that?" Trish asked.

It was an excellent question, one I had been about to ask myself. I nodded my approval to her and then turned to Gunther, waiting for an answer.

Gunther looked away for a moment and then down at his shoes before he replied. "I took off. There was no use pleading our case anymore, since it was clear the woman wasn't going to change her mind. I decided to head here and start to work on this fireplace, and the next thing

I knew, my phone was ringing and Thompson was telling me what had happened."

"So you decided to keep on working even after you learned about the murder?" I asked him,

"I couldn't very well do the woman any good at that point, now, could I?" he asked.

"And you've been here all alone since then?" Trish asked.

"I have," he answered, almost pleased with himself that he didn't have an alibi, at least not one that he cared to share with us, for the time of the murder. "Now, if you'll excuse me, I've got a little more work to do before my hands give out on me completely."

It was clear that he was dismissing us, but I wasn't quite ready to leave yet. "Since you say that you didn't kill Samantha, do you have any idea about who might have?"

"I have a few ideas, but they aren't anything I'm willing to share with you. No offense," he added. "Take my advice, and don't believe everything people tell you."

"Including you?" Trish asked him directly.

Gunther looked surprised by the idea, but he nodded and smiled. "Even me." And then he walked over to a masonry saw and flipped it on. It made a whale of a racket as he started cutting through a stone slab, and I motioned for Trish to step away.

It was clear this particular interview was over.

Once we were back at the Jeep but before we got in, I asked Trish, "What do you think?"

"I think he's having too much fun given the fact that a woman was murdered today," she said.

"I don't think Gunther takes *anything* too seriously," I told her.

"So, do *you* believe him?"

"Not until I get confirmation that he was here when he said he was," I admitted.

"What do we do, knock on doors and ask people? He's not exactly surrounded by nosy neighbors, is he?"

I glanced around and realized that no one had a good view of the front of Gunther's property. Then again, they didn't have to see him. If he'd been making that much racket all afternoon, someone had surely heard something.

"Let's try something," I said as I got into the Jeep and motioned for Trish to do the same. Once we were both safely belted in, I drove away from Gunther's place.

That is, at least until he couldn't see us anymore.

I parked the Jeep a dozen yards away, though out of sight, and got out. Trish joined me and asked, "What are we doing?"

"Trust me," I said as I knocked on Belinda Carlisle's door.

She came out with a frown, which wasn't that unusual for Belinda. "Trish, what are you doing hanging out with this troublemaking donut maker? I thought you had better taste than that."

To my surprise, Trish shot right back at one of her customers. "You might think so, but then again, at least *someone* can stand being around *me* for more than ten minutes."

I thought my investigating partner had lost her mind, especially since we were trying to get this woman to cooperate with us, but evidently, Trish knew her customer better than I did, since Belinda hadn't been in my donut shop more than twice in the past five years. "There is that," the woman answered with a slight smile. "What do you two want? I've got gingerbread cookies in the oven."

"It's a little late for those, isn't it?" I asked her. "I think of them more as Christmas cookies."

"Gingerbread is good all year long. I'm surprised you don't have a gingerbread donut at that shop of yours."

"I've tried a few variations, but I haven't been happy with the results, at least so far."

"Try doubling the molasses and adding a bit of honey instead of cane sugar," she suggested.

"That's a great idea," I answered, making a mental note to try just that.

"I know you two didn't show up on my doorstep to trade recipes," Belinda said a bit crossly, letting her curmudgeon come back out. "What do you want?"

Just then, Gunther's saw started up again. Trish asked, "How long has that been going on?"

"It feels like all blasted afternoon," Belinda complained.

"Has he taken any breaks?" I asked.

Belinda didn't even have to think about it. "It didn't start until three, but it's been constant since then."

"Are you sure about the time?" I asked her.

"He started just as my story came on television," Belinda said. "You bet I'm sure."

"Good enough," Trish said. "Thanks, Belinda."

"For what?" she asked crabbily.

"Just being the bright ray of sunshine you always are," Trish answered with a laugh.

"It's finally happened. You've lost your mind," Belinda said, with a hint of tenderness in her voice that caught me by surprise.

"Well, we both know that it was bound to happen sooner or later. See you tomorrow," Trish said.

"What makes you think I'm coming to the Boxcar Grill tomorrow?" Belinda asked her pointedly.

"If you don't, it will be the first country-style steak special you've missed in years."

"Yeah, you got me. I'll be there," she said as the timer in her hand went off. "Got to go."

Before we could even offer our good-byes, Belinda was gone, and the door was shut firmly in our faces.

"She's something, isn't she?" I asked Trish as we headed back to my Jeep.

"We've gotten to be friends over the years, and don't give me any grief about it. You're pals with Gabby Williams, and if that can happen, then anything can."

"I wasn't criticizing, I was complimenting," I told her. "You knew exactly how to handle her. If I'd been with anyone else, we wouldn't have gotten her to cooperate in a million years."

"Is that actually a compliment, Suzanne?" she asked me with a smile.

I pretended to listen to someone far off. "I didn't hear a thing. I'm sure I don't know what you're talking about."

"I'm sure you don't," she said, smiling. "Who is next on our list?"

"I'd say that was obvious enough. Let's go see what Thompson Smythe has to say."

"Do you think his story will be any different than Gunther's?" Trish asked as we got into the Jeep and drove away.

"I don't know, but I certainly want to find out," I said.

"Thompson, we'd love to chat with you a moment if you have the time," I said as he came to the door holding a thick book with a book-mark sticking out of one section.

"I'm afraid I'm rather busy at the moment," the retired attorney said, trying to back away from the door.

"This will only take a second. We heard about the fight you and Gunther had with Samantha before she died. That must have been aw-ful, hearing about it an hour later."

"It was tragic but not entirely unexpected," the retired attorney said.

"What does that mean?" Trish asked. "Did you see something?"

"What? Of course not. I'm just saying that the woman had a rather direct way of dealing with people that made her less than beloved."

"So then, what you're saying is that you didn't like her," Trish pushed.

Maybe I'd been too eager to compliment her earlier.

"I had no feelings regarding her one way or the other," he said stiffly. "What happened to her is of no concern of mine, since I didn't do it."

"What happened after the fight you had with her?" I asked, pushing the man a little harder than I normally would. He had a gruff way of putting us off that I was finding irritating, and I had a feeling that Trish was becoming a bad influence on me with her brash behavior.

"It wasn't a fight; it was a disagreement," he said.

"Okay, what happened after your *disagreement* with the murder victim?" I asked, pressing him a bit more.

"Gunther and I decided to have a cup of coffee and discuss our options, and then he went home to work on that modern Stonehenge of his. I started looking up some legal precedents in order to press our position."

"Did you have any luck?" I asked him.

"There are some interesting interpretations, but I'm afraid it is all for naught. The hunt has been canceled. Once the inn owner heard about the murder, she wanted nothing more to do with April Springs or the scavenger hunt."

"Is it legal for her to pull the offer like that?" Trish asked.

"I'm afraid it is," he replied. "Now, if that's all you need, I have things to see to."

"Where did you get that bookmark?" Trish asked him, suddenly curious about it enough to ask.

"I found it. Why?"

"It looks like one I used to have and lost. You didn't happen to find it at the Boxcar, did you? I've been looking everywhere for it."

"I don't recall, but I'm sure it's not yours. Good day, ladies."

We were about to go when I stopped and turned back to him. "One thing is odd, though."

"Only one?" he asked with the hint of a frown.

"Right off the top of my head at least. Gunther said he came straight home after the disagreement you all had. He didn't say anything at all about having coffee with you."

I saw Thompson flinch for a split second before he tried to brush it off. "The man has been getting forgetful in his old age. We had coffee, I can assure you of that."

"Where did you have it? I know you didn't come by the Boxcar while I was there, and Suzanne would have remembered you coming to Donut Hearts," Trish said plainly.

"We came here. I prefer my blend over either one of yours. Good day, ladies."

With that, he was back inside, behind closed doors.

"So, who is lying to us, Gunther or Thompson?" Trish asked me as we headed back to my Jeep.

"I have no idea. With the timeline we got from Belinda, Thompson could be telling the truth. Then again, why would Gunther lie about having an alibi? Let's go back there and ask him."

We tried, but when we got to Gunther Peale's house, he was gone, and his tools were all put away.

Evidently, that question would have to wait for another time.

There was just one more person on our immediate list of suspects we hadn't spoken with yet, someone I'd been dreading to interview, but we couldn't put it off any longer.

It was time to interview George Morris and see if our mayor had an alibi for the time of his assistant's murder.

Chapter 9

"GEORGE, DO YOU HAVE a second?" I asked my friend, who also happened to be our mayor, as Trish and I stood just outside his office door in city hall.

"It's not a great time, Suzanne," he said as he shuffled papers from one pile to another on his desk.

"This won't take long," I assured him as we stepped into his office.

"Make it dance, then," George answered a bit coolly.

"Mr. Mayor, is that any way to treat a pair of voters with an election just around the corner?" Trish asked him, clearly trying to tease him out of his funk.

"As far as I'm concerned, that's not going to be my problem anymore," he answered, not letting her ease his mood in the slightest.

"What are you talking about, George?" I asked him, taken aback by his statement.

He threw his pen on the closest pile of papers and then leaned back in his chair, running his hands through his hair. "I'm seriously thinking about giving this up," he said as he waved his hands around the office.

"Seriously? But why?" Trish asked him.

"Because I'm sick and tired of pushing papers from one side of my desk to the other. I had a full career as a cop, and now I've more than done my time as mayor. Let someone else have the headaches. As far as I'm concerned, I'm through."

I had heard the mayor threaten to quit before but never so adamantly. "You're just feeling the stress of today," I told him. "It will get better."

"Will it, though? My assistant is dead, I'm at the top of the chief's list of suspects, and now you and Trish are here to grill me about the murder too. Exactly what part of this am I going to miss?"

"You do a lot of good, and you know it," I reminded him. "We need you, Mr. Mayor."

"Well, with all due respect, I'm not sure I still care enough to do the job anymore," he answered. "Let's get this over with. Samantha and I had words. No, strike that. That's something a politician would say. We had a fight. She thought I was phoning my job in, and I told her to go stick her head in a bucket, but do you want to know something? I have a feeling in my gut that she was right. Who likes to hear the truth when it makes you look bad? I yelled at her, she yelled at me, and then she stormed off. That was the last time I saw her alive."

"Where did you go after you fought?" Trish asked him. I wanted to know that myself, but I wasn't exactly sure how to ask the question. Again, Trish was proving to be useful to my investigation. No matter how much I disliked interrogating such a good friend, it had to be done.

"I came back here and tried to make sense of this mess," he answered.

"Do you happen to know where Samantha went?" I asked him.

"To the gazebo to check on the clue there," he said glumly. "And then someone took one of your cast iron donuts and killed her."

I hated hearing how matter-of-factly he said it, but it was true enough. "I wish I could deny it, but I can't," I said simply.

George must have seen something in my expression. "Suzanne, I didn't mean it that way. Nobody thinks you had anything to do with what happened to my assistant."

"I put the cast iron donuts out on display," I said as calmly as I could, "and I didn't pay attention to whoever stole one of them and used it as a murder weapon. I'll have to live with that for the rest of my life, but I'm not going to crawl into a hole and pull it in after me. I'm going to figure out who killed her and make sure they pay for what they did."

It was an animated speech, and I wasn't one who was prone to making any kind of speeches at all.

"Are you trying to tell me something?" George asked me with the hint of a grin on his lips.

"If you quit, whoever did this wins," I told him without any humor as I headed for the door.

"Hang on a second. It's not that simple, Suzanne," George protested, but I wasn't about to give him time to talk himself back into threatening to quit again.

"It never is, Mr. Mayor."

He was still talking as I left with Trish trailing along behind me.

"That was rough," she said as she patted my shoulder lightly.

"I know, but it had to be done," I told her as I looked at my phone to check the time. "I don't know about you, but I'm beat. Can we take the rest of the day off and start again tomorrow after I close the donut shop for the day?"

"That's not a bad idea," she said, and I could see something in her glance that gave me pause.

"Trish Granger, you are not, I repeat, not to investigate this murder without me. Do you understand?"

"I just thought I might—"

"No," I interrupted.

"I was just going to—"

"No," I repeated.

"Fine, she said, shrugging her shoulders. "Tomorrow at eleven, we start back into it."

"I'm trusting you, Trish," I told her as we started to walk out of city hall together. I paused and waved at Hannahlee at her desk before Trish and I went out the door, and she returned it with a smile.

"I said I won't do anything, and I won't," Trish admonished me.

"Then what are you going to do until then?" I asked her.

"I'm going by the Boxcar to see how the ladies have gotten along without me," she admitted. "What can I say? Leaving it for the day has been tougher than I ever thought it would be."

"I understand completely," I said, and then I gave her a quick hug. "It gets better."

"Really? How long does it take? Emma and Sharon have been running Donut Hearts part-time for quite a while now, haven't they?"

"They have."

"So, when did you quit worrying about your shop when you weren't there?" Trish asked me earnestly.

"I'll let you know when and if it ever happens," I said with a shrug.

For some reason, that made her laugh. "I suspected as much. Have a good night, Suzanne."

"You too," I said as my cell phone rang. "Sorry. I've got to take this."

"Is it about the case?"

"No, it's personal," I answered.

"Go right ahead then," Trish said with a wave as she walked toward the Boxcar Grill.

When I'd glanced at my cell phone, I'd seen that Momma was calling me.

I wondered what she wanted. Was it about the case, my earlier conversation with her husband, or something else entirely?

There was only one way to find out, so I stopped putting it off and decided to go ahead and answer it.

"Hey, Momma. What's up?"

"The sky, most birds, airplanes, the moon, the stars, and a host of other things," my mother said. "Is that any way to greet your mother?"

"Sorry," I said automatically. "How are you this fine evening, Mother Dearest, and how may I serve you?"

"Your wit never tires, Suzanne."

"That's so sweet of you to say," I replied, smiling to myself that I'd nudged her a bit with my reply. After all, she wasn't the only button pusher in our family.

"It wasn't a compliment," Momma answered drolly.

"Well, I was raised to think the best of people, so I'm choosing to take it that way. Is that the only reason you called, to check up on my telephone etiquette?"

"As a matter of fact, Phillip and I would like to invite you to dinner. Jake is out of town, is he not?"

"Wow, word travels fast," I told her. "How did you hear about that already?"

"He had to break an engagement with Phillip," Momma said.

"I told you before, we pushed it, and it was fine by me," I heard my stepfather correct her in the background. "Dot, give the girl a break, would you?"

He was a bold man standing up to my mother like that, and I appreciated the effort, even if it was no doubt futile.

Momma told him, "I'm just..."

Phillip interrupted her before she could finish her thought, another dangerous move on his part. "I know you mean well, love, but try to let a few things slide every now and then, okay? You know how she is."

I wasn't quite sure how to take that, but he was on my side, so I decided to take his advice for my mother and do the same. "What are we having? You know what? Never mind. I'll be there in a few minutes."

"We look forward to seeing you," Momma said.

As I drove toward their home, I had to wonder if Phillip felt bad about turning me down earlier in the day. Trish hadn't been my first choice or even my fourth, but she was working out okay, at least so far. I had to admit that she brought her own individual set of skills to the investigation that I lacked, which was always a good thing. If I could get her to dial it back a bit when we were interviewing suspects, it would be better, but then again, that particular wish was futile, and I knew it. Trish had always been a shoot-from-the-hip kind of gal, and I didn't suspect that she'd change that for anyone, even me. Still, it felt as though the day had brought us a little closer together, which was never a bad thing. Grace and I had been best friends for what felt like forever, but after Momma, Trish was near the top.

Phillip took my coat as he met me at the door. I said softly, "You're a brave man going against her like that. Thanks."

"Don't mention it," he said just as quietly. "And I mean that literally. Don't mention it."

"Consider it done," I answered as I walked into the kitchen and headed straight for my mother. She seemed surprised that I'd hug her so fiercely, but if the bodies I'd dealt with had taught me anything over the years, it was that life was short, and you could never tell the folks you loved how you felt about them enough.

"My, what was that for?" Momma asked as we finally broke our hug.

"Do I need a reason to hug my own mother?" I asked her.

"Never," Momma said. "I do love you, young lady, even if you exasperate me at times."

"Right back at you," I replied with a grin. I took a deep breath and then smiled. "You made baked ziti."

"I did indeed," Momma said.

I smelled the air again. "And homemade bread, too. Wow, we're having a feast tonight."

"The bread is indeed homemade, and I'm the one who made it, but I did it this past weekend. This was frozen and thawed."

"I don't have a problem with that," I said, "on one condition."

"What might that be?"

"That there's butter to go along with it," I answered.

"I wouldn't own a house without butter in it," Momma said, "especially when there's homemade bread involved." She turned to her husband and added, "Before you even ask, of course you may have some butter as well. Did you note the keyword in that sentence?"

"I don't know. All I heard was butter," he answered with a grin.

"'Some.' The word was 'some.'"

"How much is some?" he asked with a frown.

"One fourth of your usual portion," Momma answered.

"Three quarters," Phillip countered.

"One eighth," Momma replied.

"Hey, that's not how you're supposed to negotiate," Phillip protested.

"I wasn't about to meet you in the middle," Momma answered as she pulled the bread out of the oven, where it had been warming along with the ziti. "Care to return to the quarter offering?"

"Sold," he said with glee. "I'll serve the salads. A fourth is still better than what I've been getting lately."

"You've done well on your diet," she said as she put the bread down and patted his cheek affectionately.

"It's been tough, but at least I don't work in a donut shop," he answered as he looked at me. "Suzanne, how do you not weigh eight hundred pounds? Everything you make there is delightful and bursting with calories."

"It's part willpower and part an aversion to buying new and bigger sizes of blue jeans," I answered honestly.

"I understand that," he said.

"I wish I'd been born with your metabolism, Momma," I told her. She was a mere wisp of a woman, tiny and petite, and I'd often wished that I'd had her ability to eat whatever she wanted to and not seem to gain a single ounce.

"And I wish I had *your* figure," Momma said.

I rubbed one index finger over the other one as I scolded her, "It's not nice to tease your daughter like that."

"I wasn't," Momma said. "I think your curves are delightful, Suzanne."

"Thanks," I said, a bit startled by the admission.

My stepfather surprised my mother by reaching from behind her and hugging her tightly. "I personally love your figure, myself," he said.

She blushed a bit as he kissed her cheek. "Oh, go on."

"Well, let's see. I suppose I could keep complimenting you, but that seems a bit needy, don't you think?" he asked with a grin.

"You know what I meant," she answered. "Now let me go, you silly old goat. I need to finish getting dinner on the table."

"Okay, but it's to be continued," he said with a smile that deepened her blush even further.

"Should I leave you two kids alone?" I asked as I started for the front door. It was pure bluff, but they didn't know it. There was no way I was leaving that bread and ziti of my own free will. "Or can you behave yourselves?"

"We can try," Phillip said with a grin.

"Don't pay any attention to him, Suzanne. For some reason, he's in a particularly good mood tonight."

"I was waiting for Suzanne to get here to tell you both at the same time. I think I figured out what happened to Zacharieth West."

"From April Springs?" I asked. "I thought his disappearance was a mystery for the ages? How long ago was it?"

"A hundred and fifty-seven years ago, and it was, until I found a reference to a Zebadiah Westin in Hickory who showed up there about the time Zacharieth disappeared," he answered as he started for the table where his clippings and photocopies were spread out in piles that only he thought of as organized. "He started a new family there, after arriving dead broke and half dead, according to the reports."

"That poses more questions than it answers," I said.

"True, but I'm on the case. I'll know the whole story before long now that I have a lead."

"Talk about cold cases," I said as I set the table for three. I missed Jake, but he was off taking care of family business, and if I had to spend time with other people, these two would do nicely.

"The truth is, that's *all* I'm allowed to do these days," he answered, a bit of a storm cloud forming on his brow.

"Phillip Martin, we agreed to discuss that later," Momma said in that Mother Voice that still managed to send chills down my back and raise the hair on my arms.

"Sorry," Phillip replied, but his sincerity was suspect as far as I was concerned. They must have had words about my earlier request for help and his forced refusal, and from the sound of things, the discussion was far from over. I wasn't about to get involved, though. It wasn't my fight, and I had enough on my hands without adding a little domestic discord to the mix.

"The table is set," I said as brightly as I could manage. "What else can I do to help?"

"Sit," she commanded, and I had no problem obeying.

Momma plated the ziti and handed me my portion. The cheese was perfectly browned on top, and I knew there were layers of deliciousness waiting for my fork to discover, but I put that aside for the moment and buttered a roll the moment she handed it to me. I honestly tried to keep my portion modest for Phillip's sake, but I'm afraid the knife had other ideas, and soon enough, the roll was slathered with more butter than even I needed. Scraping some of it off would have seemed rude though, so I pushed ahead and took a bite anyway.

It was amazing, as I knew it would be.

Momma smiled softly when our gazes met, and I gave her a thumbs-up gesture with my free hand. There was no way I was putting that roll back down until it was gone.

After dinner, I helped Phillip clean the table while Momma put the leftovers away. "Sorry if I caused any trouble earlier," I said sincerely.

"You didn't, so there's no need to apologize. Your mother needs to remember that I'm not a prized show dog. I'm a mutt who likes to get dirty."

"Are you really comfortable with that particular analogy?" I asked him with the hint of a smile.

"I am. After all, my best dogs have all been mutts," he said proudly.

"I get that," I told him, "but Momma is just asking you not to get involved out of love."

My mother chose that moment to come back out for the ziti that was left, though the three of us had put a serious dent in the original dish. "Suzanne, I can fight my own battles, thank you very much," Momma told me.

I was about to answer when Phillip beat me to it. "That's just it, Dot. There shouldn't be a fight at all. I've never asked you to give up your business dealings, have I?"

"No, but my life has never been endangered because of one of them either," Momma answered stiffly.

"Never?" I asked her pointedly. I had meant to stay out of it, but evidently, my mouth had other ideas.

"Well, hardly ever," she conceded.

"Dot, I want to respect your wishes, I truly do, but if I feel I can't be myself, what point is there in living?"

"Aren't you being a bit melodramatic?" she asked him.

I was starting to get a little uncomfortable, but there was no gracious way for me to leave.

"I'll make you a deal right here and now," Phillip said. "I'll quit investigating crime, old and new, if you sell all of your businesses and we retire together."

"You're bluffing," Momma said, clearly caught off guard by his offer.

"Try me," he answered.

After a few moments, Momma replied, "You know running my little empire is what keeps me young."

"And solving crimes is what does it for me," Phillip said.

I was about to chime in when my stepfather glanced my way and shook his head once. It killed my comment, and we stood there as Momma pondered the possibilities of what he'd just said. I would have loved to be able to do that, to just drop something until Momma had a chance to come to her own conclusion, but again, my mouth often had a mind of its own.

After an uncomfortably long time, uncomfortable for me at any rate, Momma finally spoke. "I was wrong to rein you in. Do what you need to do."

"Thank you," he said as he hugged her tightly.

"I suppose that means you'll be helping Suzanne after all," Momma said.

Two was company, but three was unwieldy, and I already had a partner. I was about to say just that as delicately as I could manage when Phillip shook his head and did it for me. "She's already made up her team. I'll catch her the next time she needs someone to back her up."

"I look forward to it," I told him.

"Just don't make it anytime soon, all right?" Momma asked me.

"You know as well as I do that I have no control over that," I told her.

"Are you making any progress with Samantha's murder so far?" Phillip asked me.

I started to answer but then glanced over at my mother. I fully expected her to put the brakes on the conversation, but she surprised me by saying, "You might as well go on. He's dying to hear, and I must admit, I'm a bit curious myself."

It seemed that whether I wanted to rehash my investigation or not, I wasn't going to have any choice in the matter. Then again, the two people who wanted to hear what I'd learned were both smart, intuitive, and insightful.

It couldn't hurt to get their points of view, and it might just help me clarify my own.

Chapter 10

"OKAY, IF YOU'RE SURE. Let's start with my list of suspects," I said as I settled into the living room near the fire. Of all the ways I'd ever have predicted I'd be spending Valentine's Day as an adult, this wouldn't even have made the top fifty. I missed Jake, but I understood he needed to be where he was at the moment, and besides, talking it over out loud with my mother and her husband might help me solve this case.

After considering that, I realized there were a lot worse things I could be doing. "It's honestly just as much about who had the opportunity to steal my strawberry cast iron donut as it was who had motive to kill Samantha. She wasn't really all that beloved, truth be told."

"I had some contact with the woman myself," Momma said, which surprised me.

"How did *your* circles come together?" I asked her.

"She applied to be my assistant," Momma admitted.

"I didn't know that," I told her, surprised by the admission.

"Neither did I," Phillip added. "It's not like you to keep things from me, Dot."

"I had over two dozen applicants for the position after you turned me down, Suzanne. I didn't realize you would both want a complete list of all of my discards."

"Ouch, that's a bit harsh," I told her. "Did you meet with all of them?"

"No. Samantha made the first cut, but she failed during the interview process," Momma admitted.

"Do you mind telling us why?" I asked her.

"She seemed a bit *too* eager to please me, if that makes any sense. She implied that the rules were not for everyone, and that if I needed her to do anything, as she put it, in the gray area, she'd have no problem with it. I push the boundaries, but I won't do anything that is overtly illegal," Momma added a bit too emphatically, especially since neither of us had accused her otherwise.

"Okay, that's helpful," I said as I turned to Phillip. "How about you?"

"I didn't even realize George *had* a new assistant until recently," my stepfather admitted. "He's got to be on your list, doesn't he?" Phillip added a bit glumly.

"I don't like it any more than you do, but he was in my shop this morning, so I can't be certain he didn't steal the donut and use it to kill Samantha, as much as it goes against every instinct and fiber of my being."

"Did he have a reason to kill her?" Momma asked me.

"She wanted his job, and I don't think she had any compunctions about how to go about getting it," I admitted.

"So George stays on the list until proven innocent otherwise," Momma said, looking a bit sad about the admission herself. "Surely he isn't the only person you're considering."

"Not by a long shot. There's Gunther Peale, Thompson Smythe, Dr. Zoey Hicks, Luke Davenport, and Gray Blackhurst, and that's just the roster so far. Each of those folks might have had a reason to be angry with Samantha *and* had access to the murder weapon."

"Unless the thief and the killer are two different people," Phillip said.

"I find that unlikely to say the least," I told him. "After all, the donut was stolen not more than an hour or two before the body was discovered."

"Unlikely, but still possible," Phillip replied.

"Very unlikely," I said with a frown. I'd never even considered the possibility that the thief might not be the murderer. Was it a valid premise, or did it just complicate matters? I'd have to consider it now, and I almost wished that Phillip had kept the theory to himself. I had enough trouble juggling the information and theories I had so far.

"You mentioned a laundry list of names, most of whom I know," Momma said. "Do you actually have motives for each of them?"

"In varying degrees," I said. "Samantha disqualified Gunther and Thompson from the contest for threatening to win it and resell the prize. When Samantha told them that wasn't allowed, evidently, there was a huge argument about it."

"Surely the two men can alibi each other," Phillip said. "I've known them both for a great many years, and I can't see either one of them killing her for a trip."

"You should know better than anybody that sometimes, people do things completely out of character in anger," I told him.

"But Phillip has a point," Momma said. "Have you had the opportunity to ask them if they have alibis?"

"Thompson swears they both went to his house for coffee right after the fight, but Gunther claimed it never happened. Obviously, one of them is lying, but which one?"

"That's troubling," Momma said.

"Let's move on," Phillip said. "Surely Dr. Hicks is beyond reproach."

"Why, because she's so pretty?" I asked him with one arched eyebrow.

"I never said she was pretty," Phillip protested.

"Come now, you'd have to be blind not to have noticed it," Momma scolded him.

"I said I never said it, not that I didn't notice," Phillip replied. "I still don't think she had any reason to kill Samantha Peterson."

"Don't be so sure," I countered. "She has been dating Luke Davenport recently, who dumped Samantha for the good doctor. Luke was complaining about Samantha not taking it well when Zoey told him not to worry about it, that she'd take care of it."

"That's not good," Momma said.

"Not only that, but she's the one who found the body. She claimed she tried to save her, but I'm not so sure," I admitted.

"You don't like the doctor, do you, Suzanne?" Phillip asked me. "Is it *because* she's pretty, some might say prettier than you?"

My stepfather must have realized that he'd made a mistake the moment the comment cleared his lips as Momma turned on him. Before she could light into him, I jumped in myself. "Hang on, Momma, the man's entitled to ask the question."

"Thank you," Phillip said, looking relieved.

"Hold on. I wasn't finished. What I was about to add was 'no matter how stupid it might be.' Sure, she's prettier than I am, but so is Grace, and Trish too for that matter, and I love them both like sisters. I never claimed to be the prom queen, but children don't run away when they see me, and I've managed to get at least two men to fall in love with me. I'm cute, not beautiful, and I'm just fine with that, truth be told. So to answer your question, no, it's not because of her looks. I don't like the woman's attitude about men. She treats them more as acquisitions than people."

"Luke is no great shakes in the looks department," Phillip countered.

"No, but he recently won a substantial amount on the lottery, so I have a feeling that makes him more attractive than he was before, at least to *some* women," I said.

"When did this happen? He actually won? Why didn't anyone tell me about it?" Phillip protested.

"If you'd turn your attention to the present instead of the past a bit more often, you would have learned it all on your own," Momma said tersely. "And don't think you're going to get away with that comment about Suzanne's appearance, either."

"It's okay, Momma."

"No, it is not, but I am willing to drop it for the moment. Do you suspect Luke as well?" Momma asked me, turning her gaze away from her chastised husband.

"If she pushed him, he might have lashed out at her," I admitted.

"Have you had a chance to ask *them* about their alibis?" Phillip asked me, clearly trying to keep the focus on the investigation and not on his earlier blunder.

"They had just broken up, though who was the dumper and who was the dumpee is still up for debate, so it's hard to prove where either one of them was at the time of the murder. They were both in my shop at the same time, so either one of them could have stolen the murder weapon while I was distracted."

"Could they have been in on it together?" Momma asked me.

"Why do you say that?" I asked.

"One of them could have distracted you while the other committed the theft," she replied.

"I don't know. That seems a bit premeditated, unless they were planning to kill her all along and the breakup story was just a ruse to cover what they did. No one had any idea that I'd be using one of my other cast iron donuts as a repository for the next clue."

"That's an issue, then. What about the last name on your list? Who is this Gray fellow?"

"He is, or I should say was, Samantha's assistant at city hall," I told them both.

"How does the mayor's assistant rate an assistant of her own?" Momma asked. "Surely there's not enough money in our budget for that."

"I never thought to ask that question," I admitted. "I don't know at the moment, but I'll find out as soon as I track Gray down."

"He's missing?" Phillip asked, perking up a bit.

"I don't suspect foul play, if that's what you're implying," I told him.

"I don't either. I'm wondering if he didn't kill his boss and then run away to escape arrest," he said. "Did you talk to the chief about him being gone?"

"I never thought to mention it," I admitted.

"Call him, Suzanne," Phillip urged me.

"I'm sure he's already discovered that the man's not around," I said.

"It won't hurt following up with him then," Phillip urged.

"Fine, I'll call him on my way home."

"Call him now," Phillip insisted.

"Why the urgency?" Momma asked him. "She said she'd do it. She'll do it."

"Neither one of you has ever been the chief of police," her husband explained. "You'd be amazed by how many good tips we got during my time holding down the job. The chief deserves all the help he can get."

"Fine," I said, taking out my cell phone to make the call I dreaded making. I was sure the last thing Chief Grant wanted was input from me, but it appeared it was the only way I was going to get my stepfather to drop it.

The police chief picked up on the eighth ring. "What is it, Suzanne? I've kind of got my hands full at the moment."

"I just wanted to talk to you about Gray Blackhurst."

I could swear I heard him stop breathing for a few seconds on the other end of the line. "What about him?"

"I tried to find him this afternoon, but it sounds as though he's missing. I just thought you should know."

"He might have been missing then, but he's not anymore," the chief said, letting out a bit of breath.

"You found him then? What did he have to say about his boss?"

Chief Grant hesitated, and then he said wearily, "That's the thing. He's not saying much of anything given the fact that he's dead."

I dropped my phone in shock, and as Momma and Phillip started peppering me with questions, I retrieved it. "What happened?"

"I'm not at liberty to discuss that at this moment. Truth be told, I probably shouldn't even have told you that he was dead. Keep that between us, okay?"

"I can't even tell my mother and Phillip?" I asked him.

After a few seconds, he sighed. "I suppose word will get out soon enough. Tell them, but that's it. Do me a favor, ask them not to spread it around just yet, okay?"

"I will," I told him. "When you can talk about it, let me know, okay?"

"Maybe," he answered, and then he hung up on me, not that I could blame him.

I turned to Momma and Phillip, wondering how to share that particular bit of bad news, but instantly, I decided that it was best told quickly, like a Band-Aid being ripped from the skin.

"One of my suspects is dead," I told them, "but you can't tell anybody."

"Which one was it? Not George?" Momma asked, her face going ashen.

"No, at least that's something. It was Gray Blackhurst."

"How did he die? Was it an accident or murder? I doubt it was natural causes. That seems like too much of a coincidence to me, coming on the heels of his boss's death," Momma said.

"That's all the chief would tell me," I said. As Phillip reached for his cell phone, I added, "Don't call him, Phillip. He's got his hands full at the moment, and he doesn't need any more outside pressure to share what he knows."

My stepfather took the hint and laid his phone back on the table beside him.

I stood and headed for the door.

"Where are you going, Suzanne?" Momma asked me.

"I need to go home," I told her.

"You shouldn't be alone tonight," she said.

"I'll be fine," I answered as I started to put my jacket on.

"The truth is that *we'd* feel better if you stayed here. If anything ever happened to you, we'd never be able to forgive ourselves for letting you walk out that door tonight," Phillip added. "Right, Dot?"

It appeared from the expression on my mother's face that Phillip had just gotten out of the doghouse for his earlier comment. "That's right."

"I appreciate it, I really do, but I'm sleeping in my own bed tonight," I told them as I kissed a cheek each.

"At least call us when you get there and you're locked safely at home," Momma said.

"Should I follow you there to make sure you get inside okay?" Phillip asked, reaching for his own jacket.

"No, you shouldn't," I said firmly.

"But you'll call?" Momma asked again.

"I'll call," I said. "Thanks again for dinner. I needed that."

"You know you are always welcome here, Suzanne," Momma said.

"That goes double for me," Phillip added.

I got out of there before they could persuade me to stay. I wanted to be back at my own place, but their concern had me jumpy when I got home. I sprinted from the Jeep to the front porch and then bolted inside after fumbling with my key a few times and then managed to lock the door solidly behind me.

I waited a few seconds to catch my breath and bring my pulse back down within reason before I was ready to talk to them.

"I'm here, I'm safe, and I'll stay that way," I told Momma when she answered before the first ring had a chance to end.

"And you're in for the night?" Momma asked me hopefully.

I glanced at the clock and saw that it was after seven, early for most folks but getting late for a donut maker who had to be up in less than eight hours. "I'm not going anywhere. Good night, Momma. I love you."

"And I you," Momma answered.

"Me too," I heard Phillip say loudly from nearby.

"I presume you heard that," Momma said.

"I did. You got yourself a good one there, you know that, don't you?"

"As did you," she replied. "Happy Valentine's Day, Suzanne."

"Right back at you," I told her, suddenly realizing that I hadn't even considered the fact that I might have wrecked Momma and her husband's plans for a romantic dinner. "Momma, I'm sorry if I barged in on *your* celebration tonight."

"Don't be silly. My sweet husband treats every day as though it were special. We don't need anyone telling us when to show it."

"Jake and I feel the same way," I said.

After we hung up, I found myself missing my husband, but I didn't want to call him. No doubt he had his hands full with his sister's woes at the moment.

I got ready for bed, and as I crawled between the empty sheets, I felt something under my pillow.

Pulling out my cell phone, I turned its flashlight on and saw that Jake had left me a note.

"Suzanne,

Sorry I'm not there with you, but this trip couldn't be helped, so thanks for understanding.

I have just one question for you.

Will you be my Valentine? Check yes or no."

There were two crudely drawn boxes below it, a large one labeled yes and a much, much smaller one beside it labeled no, and then his scrawled signature.

"Jake.

PS. If it's no, I have some serious fence-mending to do when I get back, but I'm up for the challenge.

PPS. I love you.

PPPS. I thought I said that before, but I reread my note just now and realized I hadn't. But I do. Love you. A bunch."

Like a schoolgirl with a crush, I went to sleep with that note in my hand, happy that I'd found someone to make me happier than I ever thought I could be.

All things considered, it wasn't a bad way to end the day, even if it had brought tragedy to two citizens of my small town.

Chapter 11

AS I WOKE UP THE NEXT morning, I felt something pressed against my face, and it took me a second to realize that it was the note Jake had left me the day before. Great. I'd smudged it in my sleep, wrinkled it badly as I'd tossed and turned, and now parts of it were hard to read. Pressing it out as best I could with the flat of my hand, it was better but still not great. I knew anyone else would think I'd lost my mind when I got out my iron and pressed the note, flattening it carefully so I could preserve it. Thank goodness it was two forty-five in the morning, when no one could see what I was up to, standing there at the ironing board in my pajamas, pressing a piece of paper.

It looked pretty good by the time I finished it, so I set the iron aside and laid the note carefully on the kitchen table. As I got dressed and had a quick bite to eat, I started thinking about Samantha Peterson and Gray Blackhurst. What had happened to strike down *two* members of the mayor's staff? Had something happened at city hall to put their lives in danger, or were the deaths of a more personal nature? There couldn't be anything random about them, that was for sure. I hated coincidences, and this would have been the mother of all of them, even if it turned out to be true.

I was heading for the front door when something nagged at the back of my mind. I kept thinking I'd left something undone as I scraped a light dusting of snow from my Jeep's windshield, and I was nearly to the donut shop when it hit me.

I'd forgotten to unplug the iron! I backed into Grace's driveway and turned around. As I pulled back into my driveway, I saw something that I had clearly missed earlier.

There was a set of footsteps in the snow leading up to my front porch, and I wasn't a hundred percent positive that they hadn't been there when I'd left so recently.

Apparently someone had decided to pay me a visit during the night. The question was, were they still there, lingering somewhere in the woods, or were they now inside my cottage, waiting for me to come back in?

The door was securely bolted, and I could see the steps leading off into the woods, so whoever had been there was now gone.

At least I hoped so.

There was a crude note taped to the front of the door, though.

It said simply, "STOP."

It wasn't much of a message, but it was enough to make the point.

Apparently someone was unhappy with my investigation, and they were giving me a warning.

It was just too bad that I didn't respond to things like that. They only made me more determined than ever to find what, or in this case who, I was looking for.

I went inside and thought about what I should do next after I checked my iron. I'd unplugged it after all, so the trip back hadn't been necessary.

But if I hadn't come back, I wouldn't have spotted those footprints or read the note in a timely manner. Any sane person would call the police, but did I really want them to know that I'd gotten too close to something? It could seriously impede my investigation if Chief Grant found out that someone had threatened me. Granted, there was no threat mentioned in the one-word note, but it was certainly implied. I was kind of surprised whoever had left that note hadn't added "OR ELSE," truth be told. Could it just be some kind of prank? Maybe it wasn't from the killer after all.

That was complete and utter nonsense, and I knew it.

There was only one thing I could do, so I did it.

I dialed 911 and braced myself for the consequences.

To my surprise, Darby Jones answered my call, Chief Grant's second-in-command.

"Darby, what did you do this time?"

"Suzanne, is that you? What do you mean, what did I do?"

"Every time you do something you shouldn't, you get the worst duty the chief can think of," I said, forgetting for a moment the threat I'd just found taped to my door.

"It's not like that. We're shorthanded at the moment, so we're all pitching in. Those budget cuts from Raleigh are killing us. What's up with you? I've got a feeling you didn't just call to chat with whoever was on duty."

"I found something," I admitted, but before I could explain what, Darby interrupted.

"Are you at the donut shop? I'll see you in thirty seconds."

Before I could correct him, he was gone, and when I called back, I got the police's voicemail, which wasn't all that great given that it was an emergency hotline for the community. In his haste, Darby must have forgotten to switch it to call forwarding so the next cop on duty would get the call. I started to call the chief's personal cell phone number, but then I realized I'd get Darby in trouble if I did that, so that was out.

Okay, he was a smart guy. If he drove by Donut Hearts and didn't see my Jeep, he'd come straight to the cottage.

At least I hoped that was what he would do.

I walked back out on the porch and waited. As I did, I pulled out my cell phone and took a picture of the note as well as the footprints, or at least what was left of them. Unfortunately, the wind must have kicked up since I'd been inside, and the snow had been light and powdery as it was.

I could see faint glimpses of where the prints had been, but that was about it. There was no way now to tell if a man or a woman had made them, and that looked to be true as far as I looked in the yard.

My dithering might have cost me a clue as to who had paid me a visit in the wee hours of the morning.

I just hoped that it didn't cost me more than that.

"You weren't at Donut Hearts," Darby accused me as he got out of his police cruiser a few minutes later.

"You're turning out to be quite the detective," I said, not able to keep my comment to myself. I was clearly deflecting my own earlier failing by projecting it onto Darby, which certainly wasn't fair to him. "Sorry about that. It must have rattled me more than I realized."

"What happened?" he asked.

I pointed to the door. "That."

He read the note, took some pictures of his own, and then bagged it, tape and all. After Darby studied the porch floor and the surrounding ground, he took a few more shots, but when he put his camera away, he shook his head. "I'm afraid we won't get anything from those. This snow is so powdery it's amazing whoever did it left any prints at all."

"I shouldn't have called," I said, feeling bad for causing such a fuss. "It was probably just a prank. Sorry for the trouble."

He shook his head. "I don't know about you, but I don't know a soul who would get up in the middle of the night to leave a note on your door as a gag. The message is pretty clear, isn't it?"

"What? Stop? What if they don't like donuts, and they want me to stop making them? Then again, they might not like the way I dress."

"Don't be ridiculous," Darby said with a frown.

"It's not all that crazy," I replied. "Lester Moorefield tried to get my donuts banned once upon a time, and Gabby Williams has been chiding me about wearing blue jeans for years."

"Lester is dead, and Gabby is sound asleep. We both know this is about your investigating what happened to Samantha Peterson."

"And Gray Blackhurst, too," I added.

Darby looked at me sharply. "How did you know about that? The chief has strict orders to keep that under wraps."

I wasn't about to tell him that his boss had been the one who'd told me the news. "I can't reveal my sources, Darby."

"You're not a reporter protecting the third amendment, Suzanne," he told me.

"Actually, it's the first one," I corrected him. "That's freedom of the press. The third is about housing soldiers in your house without your permission, though I'm not going to let that happen either."

"Joke if you want to, but this is serious," Darby said as he started to pull out his police radio.

"Who are you calling? Let's leave the chief out of this, can we?"

"Sorry. No can do," Darby said with a frown. "We all have strict orders to contact him day or night if you ever call in."

"I'm touched," I said.

"I wouldn't be all that warmed by it," Darby said. "Usually, when you contact us, there's trouble somewhere we need to take care of."

"I'd love to deny it, but I can't," I told him as he placed his call. I glanced at my phone to see just how late I was going to be. "Will this take long? I've got to get started making donuts."

"Maybe you'll have to skip a step or two this morning," he told me, "but this can't wait."

I resigned myself to waiting for the chief to get dressed and arrive, but evidently, he hadn't been asleep. I knew when Grace was out of town on business, he was restless, but this was crazy.

He drove up in his squad car, got out, and headed straight for Darby. "Report."

"I left the iron on, and I had to..." I started to say when he cut me off.

"Not you. Him."

I shrugged and decided not to interrupt again if I could help it. Darby told him my story swiftly and concisely, and when he was finished, the chief nodded. "Why don't you head back to the station and catch any phone calls that might come in?"

"I don't mind hanging around and helping you search the woods," Darby said as he looked around at the swirling darkness around my cottage.

"Whoever left that note is long gone," the chief said. "Besides, you forgot to forward the calls to Perkins."

"Whoops," Darby said as he hurried for his squad car. I'd wanted to protect him from that, but evidently, the chief was already aware of his slip.

"It's not his fault," I told the chief as soon as his second-in-command was gone. "He was hurrying to help me."

"There's always time to do things right the first time," the chief said, no doubt repeating something he said often.

"Not always, but I get your point. Anyway, sorry for the fuss. I probably should have just thrown the note away and ignored it."

That was evidently the wrong thing to say. The chief clearly bristled as he answered, "That would have been the exact *wrong* thing to do. This is serious, Suzanne," he said as he waved the bagged note in front of me. "You need to leave this investigation to me and my people. We are trained for this sort of thing."

"I understand that, but I can ask questions that you aren't allowed to. Besides, people like to talk to me. I've been told I'm a good listener."

"Well, evidently, *someone* took offense," he replied.

"Even if the killer wrote that note to scare me off, it's not much of a threat as warnings go, is it? In fact, it seems a bit half-hearted to me. Maybe someone didn't want me digging into their life because of something I might uncover that has nothing to do with the murders."

"Why do you assume there was more than one murder?" he asked me.

"Don't tell me Gray Blackhurst died of natural causes," I chided him. "I'm not buying it, and neither should you."

"It's officially on the books as an accidental overdose by misuse of prescription drugs at this point, at least until we can get the official autopsy report," he told me.

I was shaken to the core by his free admission. "Gray *killed* himself?"

"That's what it looks like," the chief admitted.

"Why on earth would he do that?" I asked, not able to wrap my head around the idea of someone choosing to end their own life.

"Like I said, it looks like an accident. Evidently, he took too much of the wrong drugs mixed together. What do you think, he killed himself on purpose because he was so despondent over his boss's death?"

"He wasn't in love with her, I can tell you that right now," I said firmly.

"How can you be sure? Not everyone wears their hearts on their sleeves," Chief Grant told me.

"I saw them together yesterday. *Nobody* is that good an actor." I had a sneaking suspicion that I had to air. "What makes you think it was an accident? Who told you that?"

"The coroner. She came out to the scene and checked things out so we could remove the body," the chief admitted.

"Are you talking about Zoey Hicks, the same woman who is a suspect in the earlier murder?"

"You think *Zoey* killed Samantha Peterson?" the chief asked incredulously. What was it with men's blind spots when it came to attractive women?

"Isn't she even on your list?"

"Of course she is, but I don't give it much credence," he admitted. "There are other, more viable possibilities."

"I know that," I said as something else occurred to me. "Hang on a second. If you think it was an accident, then there wouldn't be a note, would there?"

"We didn't find anything like that," he admitted.

I frowned for a second. "I wonder why there wasn't one there. That would have added a nice bow to the package, but I suppose it wasn't strictly needed."

"What are you talking about, Suzanne?"

"Don't you see? If whoever killed Samantha wanted to make it look as though Gray had done it and killed himself out of remorse, a note would have been perfect."

"Like I said, there was no note," he repeated, clearly unhappy about my possible theory.

"Maybe not on paper, but did you check his computer?"

"We're trying to, but we can't break his password," he said.

"Check his desk drawers at work and at home," I told him. "People often write them down to remind them, especially if they change them a lot."

He shrugged. "Maybe."

"It's worth a shot. Come on. I'll go to his place with you and help you look."

The chief frowned. "I thought you had donuts to make this morning. Isn't that how this whole thing got started?"

"Emma will be at the shop in twenty minutes," I said as I checked my phone again. "I can get her there now to get things started, and after we swing by Gray's place, you can drop me off at the donut shop."

"I don't know if that's such a good idea," Chief Grant said a bit reluctantly. "I wouldn't want folks to think that I can't do my job, and I have to bring in donut makers to do it for me."

"Who is going to see us at three thirty in the morning?" I asked him. "Come on, with both of us looking, we can cover twice as much ground. Besides, if we don't find it, or if we do and there's no note, no one is the wiser."

I didn't think he was going to go for it, but to my surprise, he nodded. "Fine. Get in the car."

"Yes, sir," I said.

Before he pulled out of my driveway, he hesitated.

"Come on, don't get cold feet now," I chided him.

"I just want to know one thing."

"What's that?" I asked, expecting some dark and deep question.

"Did you remember to turn your iron off?"

"Done, checked, and double-checked," I told him. "Let's go."

"I'm probably crazy for doing this, but it was your idea, so it's only fair that you get to see it through with me," he replied.

"I think so too."

"Just don't tell anyone, okay?" he asked as he drove to Gray's apartment.

"I wouldn't dream of it," I replied, still having a hard time believing the police chief was actually including me in an investigation, no matter how minor my involvement might be.

Chapter 12

"IT ISN'T MUCH, AS APARTMENTS go, is it?" I asked the chief after he pulled down the crime tape before he let us into Gray Blackhurst's apartment.

"Just wait," Chief Grant said as I followed him inside.

It turned out that mild-mannered Gray had the oddest sense of taste that I ever would have imagined. It looked as though the sixties had returned in force, exploding everywhere I looked. Walls were covered with weird psychedelic black-light posters, and instead of doors, the openings had plastic beads strung across them. There was even a small section of bright-orange shag carpeting that lay over the linoleum flooring. Peace signs in all shapes and forms were everywhere, and there was a case of vinyl records sporting covers from a bygone age. I couldn't have lived one moment in the cacophony of color, tone, and hue, but it must have suited Gray.

The chief looked at me and offered me a wry smile. "It's something, isn't it?"

"I don't have words," I told him as I tried to pull my gaze from the décor. "Where did you find him?"

"He was in there," Chief Grant said as he pointed to the small bathroom. "You don't need to see that, do you?"

"No," I said, glad that at least I wouldn't have to be in the same room where someone had so recently died, under mysterious circumstances at best. "There's no need for that."

"Okay. His office is in here," the chief said as he led me into a small alcove that was barely bigger than a closet. "This is supposed to be a two-bedroom unit, but I don't know who would ever call this a bedroom."

The décor followed in there as well, and I half expected to find a beanbag chair instead of a standard one, but Gray had kept to modern convention, in at least that respect.

"We brought the computer back here after we couldn't crack it," the chief said. "Have a look around and see if you're right about his password."

I started pulling open the drawers of his plain metal desk, hoping to see something taped to the sides that gave us a clue how to get into his computer.

There was nothing along those lines, but the drawers were stuffed with office supplies. I saw a few marked with "city hall property" on them. "He stole office supplies from work," I said, mostly just a comment on the fact.

"Well, it's a little too late to arrest him for that," the chief said. "Anything else?"

"Not yet," I said as I methodically started pulling items out, looking underneath them for the errant password.

I found one slip that looked promising.

"Find something?" the chief asked me.

"Maybe," I said as I turned the computer on and tried typing in the password I'd found, "Grayismyfavoritecolor."

The main screen didn't respond to it.

"That was a bust," I said as I set it aside.

"Keep looking," the chief said.

I did as he asked and found three more passwords, "GrayMenarec00l," "Greyisntrite," and "GrayDaysgoneforever."

None of them unlocked the main screen.

"I don't get it," I said. "How can *none* of these be the right passwords?"

"Maybe they're for bank accounts or websites or something like that?" the chief asked. "He wouldn't necessarily have to change his login password very often, would he?"

"Maybe not," I said, beginning to wonder if my guess had been wrong. I had started putting things back into place when I dropped a refill for his Scotch tape. The cylinder landed sideways and rolled toward the drapes, and as I got down to retrieve it, I saw something that caught my eye.

It was a crumpled piece of paper wedged in the folds of the drapery. It wouldn't be found unless someone opened the drapes, which clearly hadn't happened yet. Then again, the man's body couldn't have been discovered until after dark, and we were there so early that the sun was hours away from coming up. If I hadn't found it, no doubt the next people on the scene would have, so I considered myself lucky that this just might be a clue after all.

The paper, once opened, had one long nonsense word written on it. "Heyheygraygray82."

I typed it into the computer, and sure enough, the screen opened to a letter, evidently the last thing that had been on the display.

"I can't handle what I've done.

It's just not groovy, man.

She pushed me too far.

I warned her, but she wouldn't stop pushing.

Push, push, push.

Push.

I couldn't let the Man put me down like that.

Or the Woman.

And now I can't take it back.

At least it's over now.

Peace Out."

The chief looked over my shoulder. "So, that clears that up."

"Do you really think so?" I asked.

"It's clearly a suicide note, Suzanne," he said as he took a screenshot of it with his phone. "It was no accidental overdose at all."

"Mind if I take a picture too?" I asked as I did anyway.

He didn't protest, so I considered that a small victory.

"You have any doubt that it's authentic?" he asked me, clearly troubled by the implication that it might not be legit.

"Did you dust for fingerprints when you found this?" I asked the chief.

"It was so smudged there was no way to get anything off it," he answered. "It happens sometimes."

"Could it have been done deliberately?" I asked him.

"Of course it could have," he admitted. "You don't think Gray Blackhurst wrote that note, do you?"

"I do not," I said.

"Give me one reason why. The tone of it matches his apartment, you can't deny that."

"A little too on the nose, in my opinion. Did you ever speak to the man?" I asked him.

"Maybe once or twice in passing, but the truth is that he never made that big of an impression on me."

"Exactly. I spoke with him yesterday, and that note doesn't sound like *anything* he'd ever write," I told him. "It lacks his cadence and rhythm. He might have loved the sixties, but he *never* would have written anything like that."

"Come on, he was distraught, leaving a note for the world confessing to murder. It's understandable if it doesn't sound as though he were in his right mind."

"Maybe, but then why was the password crumpled up and thrown away?" I pushed on.

"He could have just changed it and needed the reminder to sign back on," he said. "Once he was on, he threw it away. It's not like he was ever going to need it again."

"What if someone else did it?" I asked.

"Why would someone kill him and then make it harder for us to see the red herring they planted?" the police chief asked.

It was a fair question.

Unfortunately, I didn't have an answer for him.

"None of this makes sense," I said after a moment or two of silence.

"There we agree," the chief said. "But these things often don't, and I shouldn't have to remind you of all people of that."

I shrugged and glanced over at the small printer nearby. It was off, so out of curiosity more than anything else, I flipped it on, and to our surprise, it started to print something.

It was the suicide note.

"There you go," the chief said. "That explains everything."

"I don't see how," I said as I looked at the paper. "Why wouldn't he wait to kill himself until AFTER the suicide note printed out?"

"How should I know? Maybe he took the pills first and then decided to leave the note. He must have misjudged the dose, and he was dead before he could do it," the chief said. "Suzanne, you are reaching, and you know it."

"What about the warning I got this morning, and the footprints?" I asked him, not willing to give it up just yet. "Surely you haven't forgotten about that already. You and Darby are the ones who made such a fuss about it in the first place."

"It was a prank, nothing more," the chief said.

"I didn't think you believed that," I reminded him.

"Hey, I'm not afraid to change my mind. We know that Gray didn't leave it. He was already dead by the time you got it. Let's face it. Some of the older kids around here don't have anything better to do with their time than tweak their elders, which, sad to say, includes you. Remember the crop circles they made in Old Man Marston's cornfield?"

"That was because he ran them off from stealing apples from his orchard," I reminded him.

"Yeah, and how many kids have you kicked out of Donut Hearts for being rowdy or doing something you didn't approve of?"

"A few," I admitted, "but not in a while."

"So, maybe they wanted to wait until you forgot about them," the chief said.

"I still don't think any of it makes sense," I said as I frowned at the now-silent printer.

"I can't do anything about that," he said as he flipped the switch off. "Come on. I'll give you a ride back to Donut Hearts."

"We're not finished here yet though," I protested.

He raised an eyebrow. "We?"

"You know what I mean. We can't just accept this as the truth without more proof."

Chief Grant shook his head. "I'm sorry, but we don't have much choice. Now come on, I need to wrap things up here, and I can't do that until I get you back to Donut Hearts."

"Don't bother. I'll walk," I said as I headed for the front door.

"Suzanne, don't be that way," the chief said, his voice pleading a little with me.

"What way is that?" I asked.

"You know exactly what I'm talking about," he insisted. "This isn't personal. It's business."

"That's where we differ," I told him before starting back to the shop. I glanced back and saw that he was truly hurt by my actions, and I couldn't allow that to stand. What if something happened to him and that was the last exchange we ever had? That wasn't something I was willing to live with for the rest of my life. I walked back to him and explained. "I've got a lot going on right now, the morning isn't that cold, and the shop isn't very far away. You've got things to do here, especially since we found that note. Don't worry, Stephen, I'll be fine."

He seemed to be touched by me using his first name, something I rarely did when he was on duty. After all, we'd been friends long before he'd married Grace or even become our chief of police. I knew I had a habit of being a bit harsh at times with people who disagreed with me, and it was something I was working on, but evidently, I wasn't quite there yet.

"I really don't mind. Besides, if something happened to you on the walk to the donut shop, Grace would kill me."

I grinned at the thought of him being more concerned about how his wife would feel than the end of my life. "I won't haunt you if something happens to me, and that's a promise."

"Sorry, that's not good enough," he said as he folded the printed note and tucked it into his jacket pocket. "Come on. We could have been there by now if you hadn't argued with me." He offered the hint of a smile to show me that he was just teasing, and I decided to accept it as graciously as I could.

"Who's arguing? Let's go," I told him, returning his smile.

We didn't say much on the short ride to Donut Hearts, but the tension that had been between us was now mostly gone. We each clearly believed that the other one was wrong, but we weren't going to let that affect our friendship, which was just fine with me.

The police chief might be ready and willing to write this off as a murder and delayed suicide out of remorse, but I wasn't buying it.

Not for one second.

As soon as Trish came by the donut shop after I closed it for the day, we were going to keep digging into what had happened to Samantha Peterson and now Gray Blackhurst as well.

Chapter 13

"GOOD MORNING, SUZANNE," Emma said when I walked into the kitchen. At least she hadn't seen me arrive with the police chief. I hadn't been sure how I was going to handle the conversation we were about to have about my absence, but Emma solved it for me. "Don't beat yourself up about sleeping in. I do it all the time when I'm not working, and I can't tell you the number of times I had to break the speed limit just to make it here on time."

"You shouldn't take any chances just to keep from being late," I told her, happy to let her assumption stand. I didn't want Ray Blake to have any idea what I'd been up to. If he knew that I'd been at a crime scene, or at least a potential one, with Chief Grant, the next thing I knew, it would be on the front page of his rag of a newspaper, and that wouldn't be good for the chief or me.

"Who would ever know? I'm usually the only one on the streets at 4 a.m."

"*I'll* know. Promise me you won't speed any more to get here on time," I insisted.

"I promise," she answered. "If you want to take this over, I can tackle those dishes. It's funny, but you're coming in just a few minutes before I normally do."

I looked and saw that she'd already made the cake donuts for the day. They were iced and on their trays, waiting to be taken out front, and she was just starting the yeast donuts, the second part of every one of our donut-making days. I knew places that offered cake donuts only and yeast donuts only, but I'd never done it at Donut Hearts. Sure, they were both basically the same thing—round, bready treats—but to a connoisseur such as myself, they were worlds apart. Yeast donuts were light and fluffy inside with a golden crust on the outside. When they were hot out of the fryer and freshly glazed, they practically melted in the mouth. The main way to get different flavors from them was either through the icing, or the filling if they lacked the holes. Cake donuts, though they started out with the same basic recipe every time, were often flavored at the batter stage with tidbits and flavorings added directly to the mix. They were also available to ice in different flavors as well as fillings to the whole donuts, so all in all, only the imagination limited the types and kinds of donuts I served at my shop.

"Tell you what," I said. "Why don't you make the yeast donuts and I'll get started on the dishes? It's only fair that you get to see everything through, especially after doing such a great job on the cake donuts for me." As I gathered the nearby dirty dishes, I glanced at one of the trays holding completed cake donuts. "What are these?"

"I tried something new," she admitted. "I hope you don't mind."

"I'm always willing to experiment," I told her.

When I glanced over at her, she had one eyebrow raised. "Really?"

"Okay, not always, but sometimes," I corrected myself. The cake donuts in question had a definite orange tint to them, but there were small chunks of something in the donuts as well. "Let me guess. Orange for sure."

"That part's easy," she said. "What else?"

"Can I break one apart?" I asked her.

"Sure, if you don't think you can solve it without cheating." Emma laughed.

"Okay, no breaks. I'm going to pick one up, and don't try to say that's against the rules too."

"I wouldn't dream of it," she said with a frown. Clearly she'd been about to say just that, but I'd stolen her thunder.

Once I held the donut in my hand, I could see what the chunks were. "Pineapple? Really?"

"I figured if an orange-pineapple cake could be delicious, why not try it with a donut? I got the idea from Hilda over at the Boxcar Grill."

I smelled it for a moment. "I like the spices. Let's see, there's cinnamon, some nutmeg, and is that allspice too?"

"Yes," Emma admitted. "I didn't think you'd catch that."

I tapped my nose and smiled. "Don't mess with the donut queen."

"Taste it," Emma urged me.

I took a bite and was immediately struck by the overwhelming spice presence. It was all I could do not to make a face as I bravely chewed and swallowed the bite I'd taken.

Evidently, Emma had been watching me more closely than I thought. "There's clearly too much of something. Where did I go wrong?"

"Trust the orange and pineapple more," I told her. "It doesn't need all of the spices you used, or even the quantities of the ones that might be good. The truth is, all I can really taste is the allspice," I told her. "It's too savory and bitter for what should be a sweet donut."

I wasn't sure how Emma would react, but she seemed to take it rather well. "Thanks. Great notes. That's all good to know."

She started to pitch the dozen donuts she'd made with her new recipe when I stopped her. "Hang on a second."

"Why? We clearly can't sell these," she said.

"No, but let's try something. I have a few customers who claim that my donuts are flavorless, though they keep coming back for more. I want to test them on my complainers to see if they change their tunes."

"Let me guess. You're thinking about Mattie Jones and Seth Lancaster, aren't you?" Emma asked.

"Right on both counts," I said.

"What if they don't come in today?"

"If they haven't shown up by ten, we'll call them and tell them we made donuts just for them and that they are on the house if they give us their honest opinion," I said with a grin.

"You are a wicked, wicked woman, Suzanne Hart," Emma said, though she clearly approved of my idea.

"What can I say? I like to give my customers what they ask for."

As I worked, I realized that there was something therapeutic about washing dishes and letting Emma handle the yeast donut dough. I could get lost in the suds and let my mind wander, though it didn't venture far from the murder, and possibly murders, we'd experienced in town the day before. The chief might be satisfied that Gray had taken his own life in remorse for killing his boss, but I didn't buy it for one second. That supposed suicide note hadn't sounded like the man to me, and the fact that someone had tried to scare me off my investigation didn't fit either.

I was still musing about it when Emma caught my attention. "I need to wash up. It's time for our break."

"You finished the dough already?" I asked, amazed at how quickly the time had passed.

"You should talk. You've washed everything in sight."

I looked down to see that it was true. In fact, I'd been washing the last bowl for the past few minutes, trapped by my musings about murder. "I guess that means we're ready for our break. In or out?" I asked her as I emptied the sink and dried my hands.

"You shouldn't even have to ask. Out," she said firmly. "You know the rule. Unless it's freezing and raining too, we go outside to get away for a few minutes every morning we work here together."

"At least we've got coffee," I said.

Emma frowned. "Actually, I made hot chocolate. I can whip up some coffee for you if that's what you really want."

"Hot chocolate sounds perfect," I told her.

She even added a few mini marshmallows on top, just the way I liked my cocoa.

Once we'd bundled up and grabbed our drinks, we went outside to the area where some of my braver customers liked to eat their donuts year-round, whether in the scorching heat of summer or the frigid temperatures of winter.

We were enjoying our cocoas and having a nice chat when it was all suddenly spoiled by the appearance of Ray Blake, the perennial thorn in my side.

"Dad, you shouldn't be here," Emma said as she stood to confront her father. He'd come between us more than once in the past, and Emma and I had promised each other not to let it happen again.

"I'm not here to ask questions," he said defensively.

"Well, you're too early for donuts, Ray, unless you'd like to sample one of our new orange-pineapple treats," I said with a straight face.

Emma held her expression for a second before laughing, which made me join in.

"Did I just miss something?" Ray asked as he looked from his daughter to me with a confused look on his face.

"Don't worry about it," Emma said. "If you're not here to grill Suzanne, then why are you here? You know the rules."

"I just wanted to share something with her that she might find useful to her investigation," Ray said. "But if you'd rather not hear it, Suzanne, I'll be on my way."

He had turned to go when my curiosity got the better of me. "Hang on a second, Ray. What is it?"

"Are you certain you want to hear it, especially from me?" he asked, gloating a bit that he knew something that I didn't.

"You know what? You're right. I don't. See you around, Ray," I told him smugly.

Emma protested, "Daaaaad."

He frowned for a moment. "Sorry about that. Suzanne, I've got news you can use."

"Again, not interested," I said as I stood and started back into Donut Hearts.

Before I could get in the door, Ray shouted out, "Gray Blackhurst killed Samantha Peterson, and then he killed himself!" He said it triumphantly, as though he'd just solved the crime of the century.

I didn't even miss a step, since it had been what I'd expected him to say anyway.

When I looked back outside, I saw that Emma was reading her father the riot act, and I was glad that I wasn't in his shoes. I took those few moments of solitude to make a phone call that needed to be made, though I wasn't particularly happy about being the one who had to make it.

"Chief, do you have a second?" I asked him when he picked up my call.

"Suzanne, I'm not changing my mind. You're jumping at shadows. Gray Blackhurst killed his boss and then took his own life. That's the official conclusion the police department has reached."

"But you haven't announced that to the world yet, right?" I asked him.

"No, of course not. I don't hold press conferences like that. I'll give Ray Blake a call around nine and bring him up to speed."

"You shouldn't bother," I told him. "Someone's already beat you to it."

"That's impossible," Chief Grant said. "Nobody but my staff knows about that note, unless *you* told someone."

"You know better than that. Chief, you've got a leak in your department. That's the reason I'm calling. I thought you'd like to know."

He paused and then let out a heavy sigh. "Of course I need to know. You don't have any idea who told Ray, do you?"

"If I did, I'd share it with you," I told him. "Still, you should be able to narrow it down."

"I've got an idea who told him," the chief said, "and if I can get confirmation that it's true, somebody's about to wish they'd never been born."

"It's not Darby, is it?" I asked, hoping that his second-in-command hadn't done something stupid enough to get himself fired.

"Darby? No, of course not," the chief said. "I'll handle it, Suzanne. Thanks for the heads-up."

"You're welcome," I said as I heard the front door open. "Gotta go. Donuts to make and all of that."

"Get back to it, then," the chief said.

Emma came back into the kitchen, frowning. "I told him to keep his wild speculations to himself from now on, Suzanne, but I can't make any promises."

"Emma, nobody expects you to keep your father in check," I told her sympathetically. "I don't want you to jeopardize your relationship with him for me."

"That's the thing, though. He's risking my relationship with you by coming by and saying such wild things. I won't have it."

"I'm not entirely sure he doesn't have a reason to say what he said," I told her, trying to say something to ease the stress between the daughter and her father.

"What? It's actually true?" she asked me.

"I don't believe it, but some folks do, and more will soon enough," I told her.

"I knew you would be digging into what happened to Ms. Peterson," Emma said.

"How did you know that?"

"Come on, Suzanne. The killer stole one of your cast iron donuts and used it as a murder weapon. How could you *not* dig into the case?"

"I might be asking a few questions around town," I admitted, "but it's nothing official."

"Your investigations never are, are they?" she asked me with a grin. "Forget I said that. In fact, I'm going to ignore the fact that you just confirmed that you were on the case. No one, and I mean no one, will ever hear it from me."

I hugged her, and she returned it fiercely.

"Are we good?" Emma asked once we broke our embrace.

"We're better than good. We're golden," I told her. "Now let's get back to donuts. They are uncomplicated enough, and thank goodness for that."

As she started back on the yeast donuts, she paused to grin at me. "I can't believe you were going to offer my dad one of those donuts."

"Was it too much?" I asked her.

"I just wish I could have kept a straight face," she replied with a wicked grin of her own. "Man, I would have loved to see his expression when he bit into one of those flavor bombs."

"Don't despair. Hopefully, we'll be able to see Maggie and Seth try them," I replied as I started putting clean bowls and utensils away.

"I can hardly wait," she said.

It felt good being the number-two baker in the kitchen, but only as a change of pace to our normal routine. As I watched Emma work, as covertly as possible, of course, I had to bite my tongue several times to keep from telling her that wasn't the way I did it. Instead, I tried to see why she did things the way that she did and see if I could improve my own donut-making techniques.

By the time we were ready to open, my jaw was sore from keeping it clamped so tightly shut. The morning had felt as though it had lasted for a few days, and that wasn't even taking my early soiree with the police chief into account.

I was, in the end, first, last, and always, a donut maker and not a dishwasher.

It had been an interesting experiment seeing it from Emma's perspective but not one that I cared to repeat, at least not for a very long time.

Chapter 14

"TRISH, YOU KNOW I HAVE to work this morning, right?" I asked my friend as I opened the front door for my customers sharply at six a.m.

"I know that, but we need to talk, Suzanne," she said.

"Let me take care of these folks first, and then we will," I answered as a few of my regular customers came into the shop, each of them glancing at us curiously as they walked past. Hey, it was a small town, and *all* of us had been known to eavesdrop from time to time, even me.

After I had my early birds taken care of, I turned to Trish, who had been standing rather impatiently to one side.

"Suzanne, you're not going to..." she started before I interrupted.

"Hold on," I told her as I held a finger up in the air in her direction.

Trish nodded, though clearly frustrated with me stopping her again before she could tell me what was so urgent.

"Emma, can you watch the front for a few minutes?" I asked my assistant after opening the kitchen door and looking in.

"Sure thing," she said as she walked past me. "What's up, Boss?"

"Trish came by," I answered as the diner owner nodded her greeting to my assistant.

"Shouldn't you be at the Boxcar?" Emma asked her cordially.

"Hilda and Gladys are taking over for a few days," Trish answered.

"Every week?" Emma asked her.

"No. Of course not. It's just this once," Trish said a bit brusquely. "It's an experiment."

"And from the sound of it, it's going swimmingly," Emma replied with a slight grin as the door closed behind her.

"You were a little curt with her just now, weren't you?" I asked Trish once we were alone in back of my shop.

"Sorry. There was just something I had to tell you, and it couldn't wait."

"What, that Gray Blackhurst is dead, supposedly by his own hand, and that he confessed to killing Samantha before he did it?" I asked her.

"How did you know that, and what do you mean, 'supposedly'?" Trish asked me. "Somebody already told you about it?"

"Yes," I answered.

"Now who's being short?"

"Trish, I was asked not to reveal my source."

"Not even to me, your partner in this investigation? Or am I just *supposedly* your partner and not really? You never answered my question, by the way. Why did you say 'supposedly'?"

"I don't think he killed Samantha Peterson, and I don't believe he killed himself, either," I told her.

"Based on what, exactly?" Trish asked.

"Listen to this and see if it sounds like the man to you," I said as I pulled out my cell phone and read the suicide note to her.

"First of all, I didn't know the man, so I couldn't say if that sounded like him or not, but second, how did you get a picture of that suicide note?"

I just shrugged. "I can't say."

"You can't, or you won't? Suzanne, if you don't trust me, and I mean one hundred percent, maybe you were right to threaten to fire me before. Maybe we should end this investigation right now."

Trish started for the door, and there was no doubt in my mind that she was dead serious about walking away. I thought about it for a second, and then I realized that she was right. It was either all or nothing, and I'd have to put my trust in her. "Chief Grant told me at my cottage this morning before I even made it to the donut shop, but you can't tell anybody about it." I realized how it must have sounded the second the confession was off of my lips. "Trish, what I mean is—I didn't mean—the truth is..."

My friend decided to end my struggle to find the right words. "I know you aren't having an affair with the police chief, so you can stop stammering any time."

"Of course I'm not. Why would he? He's got Grace," I said.

"Why would *you*, is the right question. After all, you've got Jake."

"True enough," I said. "The reason he was there was because I got a note this morning taped to my door, and in a moment of weakness, I called 911. Darby answered the call, and he told the chief, and that was why he was on my doorstep in the middle of the night."

"You mean you got one too?" Trish asked me as she opened her jacket and pulled out a folded sheet.

It was identical to the one I'd gotten, with its one-word admonition.

STOP.

Really, it was enough.

It appeared that I wasn't the only person being warned off the case.

"That's the main reason I came by," Trish admitted. "I heard about Gray on my way over here, but the only thing I wanted to tell you about before that was finding this taped to my front door."

"Of your place or the Grill?" I asked her.

"It was at home. Why, does that matter?"

"It could be a message from the killer that they know where we both live and how to get to us if they want to," I said, feeling a shiver run down my spine.

"When exactly did Gray kill himself, if that's really what happened?" Trish asked.

"That's an excellent question, one I had myself, but I couldn't get an answer out of the police chief."

"So, he let you take a photo of the note, but he wouldn't tell you when the body was discovered? That seems an odd fact to hold back to me."

"I was in Gray's apartment when we found the note, so it's not that odd," I explained.

"Suzanne, why is it that every answer you give me just raises half a dozen more questions? Why were you there?"

"I was helping look for Gray's password to his computer," I admitted.

"I take it you found it if that note is any indication."

"I did, but it wasn't where I thought it might be. It was crumpled into a ball and thrown across the room. I found it trapped in the draperies, of all places."

Trish frowned. "Why would Gray do that? As a matter of fact, if someone else killed him, why wouldn't they want the note to be found? None of this makes sense."

"I agree," I answered.

"What does Chief Grant think?" Trish asked.

"He believes Gray killed Samantha in a fit of rage and then was so remorseful over it that he killed himself."

"How did he do it, if you don't mind my asking?"

"Evidently, he took an overdose. The chief thinks that he took the pills first and *then* decided to write his suicide note. Gray could have changed his computer password recently, so after he was logged on, he crumpled the password up into a ball and threw it away, or at least tried to. There was a trashcan nearby if that matters. He wrote the note, started to print it out, and then the pills did their job, and he was gone."

"What makes you think he was trying to print it out?" she asked me.

"I saw the printer and turned it on, out of curiosity more than anything else, and the note printed out," I admitted.

"So, your theory is that Samantha's killer tried to frame Gray for the murder after killing him. They forced him to take the overdose, and then once he was unconscious, they wrote a suicide note and then tried to print it out but failed for whatever reason."

"That's my working hypothesis," I said, "but it still doesn't explain the discarded password."

Trish thought about that for a few seconds before smiling. "I've got it."

"Care to share it with me?" I asked.

"The killer used the password sheet to get onto the computer after killing Gray and then got rid of the evidence. After all, if the system was locked up, when the police finally figured out how to crack the password, they'd find the note there and no obvious means of putting it there without having access to the computer."

"That might work to answer one of our questions, but why did they try to print the letter if their intention was to leave it hidden?" I asked.

"Maybe they had a change of heart and decided that nobody might ever be able to crack the password, so they wanted a backup plan," Trish offered.

"Then why leave the password there? Why not just take it with them?"

"They wanted the cops to find the password all along," she said. "They just didn't want to make it too easy on them."

In a way, it all made sense, but I knew there were at least half a dozen other scenarios that made just as much sense too. "I suppose it's possible."

"We'll find out once we track the killer down," Trish said with an air of determination.

"Does that mean you don't want to quit?" I asked her.

"Are you kidding? I don't know about you, but the two STOP signs we got this morning make me more determined than ever to find out who killed Samantha. How about you? It's not like you to get cold feet, Suzanne."

"I didn't. I don't. No cold feet here," I said. What was suddenly so wrong with my basic ability to form a cogent sentence? Maybe I was still shaken by the second death so close on the heels of the first one.

Then again, it could have been the mere thought that I might ever cheat on my husband, especially with the police chief. I knew that Grace was head over heels in love with the man, but I thought of him more as a little brother than any kind of possible romantic interest.

"Okay then. Let's press on," she said.

"Agreed. And remember, don't tell anyone where we got our information," I reminded her.

"My lips are sealed. I don't think we should let anyone else know that I got a threatening note too. Does that make sense? We don't want to give the police any more reason than they already have to ban us from digging into this case."

I nodded. "It would take more than they've got to keep me away, but there's no sense in exacerbating the situation."

"Cool. So, what's next?"

I looked at the clock. "Well, I'm going to run Donut Hearts until eleven, then I'm going to clean up the shop, run my reports, lock up, go make my deposit, and then maybe grab a bite to eat before we get started untangling this mess. Can you cool your jets until then?" I asked her.

"I can, but it's not going to be easy," she answered.

"Nothing worth doing usually is," I replied.

"So, I'll come back at eleven," Trish said.

"Make it eleven fifteen, and that's only if the cash total matches the report."

"Eleven it is," she said with a grin. "If you need help massaging the numbers to make them match, I'm your gal."

"As much as I appreciate the offer, I'll be fine on my own," I told her. "See you later."

"I'll be here," Trish said and then glanced down at one of the spicy donuts Emma had made. Before I could warn her off, she took a healthy bite of one and then promptly spit it out into her hand.

"What *was* that thing?" she asked as she hurried to the sink, cupped her hands under running water, and then took a healthy swallow.

"What's the matter, don't you care for it?" I asked her as sweetly as I could manage.

"No offense, but that donut would take the hide off a rhino," she answered.

"That wouldn't be much fun for the rhino," I admitted. "Emma and I were playing around with flavors this morning." There was no reason to throw my assistant under the bus. Besides, I was a firm believer that the buck, even the donut, stopped with me.

"I'd keep playing if I were you," she said as she wiped her mouth one last time.

We had just ten of the spicy donuts left, but it had been worth sacrificing one to Trish.

Maybe next time she'd ask first, but I doubted it.

Trish was a full-speed-ahead kind of gal, a ready–shoot–aim person if ever there was one. It was normally one of the reasons I loved her, but when it came to our investigations, it definitely complicated matters.

Still, her approach had its advantages.

As long as we managed to keep it from getting us both killed.

It was nearing ten o'clock, and I was waiting on a customer when Seth Lancaster walked into Donut Hearts. I'd forgotten all about him, but him showing up like that out of the blue jogged my memory.

"Seth, how are you?" I asked as sweetly as I could manage given the man's normal dour attitude.

"Well, I'm not dead, so that's something, anyway," he said gruffly as he scanned the cases of donuts, searching for what, exactly, I couldn't say.

"Don't you ever make anything with some taste to it, Suzanne?" Seth asked with a frown.

"As a matter of fact, we've got a new donut we're still playing with, but I don't think you'd like it. It might be too much for you to handle."

"Is that a challenge? Bring me one. Anything you can make, I can take," he said defiantly.

"I don't know, Seth. I'd hate for you to be unhappy with one of my donuts." That was a real joke, because unless he had his grandkids in tow and he was buying treats for them, none of my offerings were good enough, at least in his mind.

"Suzanne, I insist."

"Okay, then. Let me grab one from the back."

I ducked back into the kitchen and grabbed one of the remaining ten donuts. "Seth is here, and he's insisting on trying one of your orange-pineapple-allspice bombs."

Emma matched my grin with the hint of a frown. "Are we really going to go through with it? I thought we were just joking around about it."

"Come on. He practically begged me for one," I told her. "You don't have to come if you don't want to, but I'm dying to see how he reacts."

"Fine, I'm right behind you. Just don't tell him *I'm* the one who made them," Emma said.

"I'd be honored to take credit," I told her as I shoved the door open.

I presented it to Seth with a bit of flair. "Listen, you can still back out if you want to. Nobody will think any less of you."

"I'm not afraid of a *donut*," he said sharply. Seth picked the treat up and bit it in half, chewing and swallowing before he could even taste it. I braced myself for his protest, but he surprised me by smiling. "Wow, that's not half bad," he said, and then he ate the remaining piece in his hand.

"Seriously?" I asked him. "You *like* it?"

"The truth is that it's the *first* thing I've had here that I could actually taste," he answered. "How many are left? I'll take a dozen right off the bat."

"There are only nine left from that run," I admitted.

"Then I'll take nine, but I'll pay you for an even dozen if you promise to make them for me every week. What do you say? Is it a deal?"

I wasn't about to turn down a standing order, even for those atrocities. A nice chunk of my business came from preorders, and it was especially welcome in the slow months at the shop. "It's a deal," I told him. "Emma, would you get Seth his donuts?"

"I'm on it," she said, shooting through the kitchen door as though she were on fire.

I rang up the sale, and Seth frowned. "You aren't charging me enough."

"You didn't get a full dozen," I told him.

"Then throw a few of those lemon-filled ones in the box."

"I didn't think you liked *any* of my donuts," I told him as I did as he instructed.

"Those aren't for me. They're for Reggie."

"Your *dog*?" I asked him with a frown.

"I use the filling to get him to take his pills," Seth answered. "You don't think I'd actually eat those myself, do you?"

Suddenly, I didn't feel so bad about teasing Seth with those overpowering donuts.

After all, in the end, he'd liked them—loved them if his reaction was any indication.

I would probably even charge him a little extra, just to make him pay a jerk tax for telling me that my donuts were good enough only for his dog usually, not him.

I didn't normally like to do that, but he'd earned it.

Once he was gone, Emma turned to me incredulously. "He liked them? He really liked them?"

"Apparently," I told her. "I hope you wrote the recipe down, because it appears we'll be making those for the foreseeable future."

"No good deed goes unpunished, does it?" she asked me.

"Or, apparently, bad ones either," I replied.

Chapter 15

"SUZANNE, ARE YOU MAKING any progress on your murder investigation?" Gabby Williams from next door asked me a few minutes before I was set to close. I didn't have any customers at Donut Hearts, and I'd sent Emma on her way an hour before, since I'd asked her to come in early and cover for me. She hadn't even put up a modest protest, so I knew she appreciated the time off. With her crazy schedule of work at the donut shop, school, and getting Barton's restaurant ready to open—which was taking forever because nobody could agree on anything—I was just thrilled she'd agreed to stay on and work with me. I knew her days at Donut Hearts were most likely numbered, but I couldn't bring myself to think about the possibility of life there without her. She'd left the shop briefly once, a time that had turned into a disaster, but I knew that soon enough, she'd be leaving me for good.

"What makes you think I'm doing anything of the sort?" I asked Gabby as I flipped the sign and locked the door behind her.

"Am I your captive now?" Gabby asked with an arched eyebrow.

I unlocked the door and held it open for her. "No, ma'am. You're free to leave. Have a nice day."

"Close that door, young lady," Gabby ordered.

I did my best to suppress my grin as I did just that, locking it yet again. I knew she'd been fussing about nothing, but I was in that kind of mood, so I'd called her on it. Not many folks in April Springs had the guts to call Gabby Williams on anything, but oddly enough, I'd become one of them.

"Make up your mind, would you? I've got work to do," I said with a grin to show her that I was just teasing.

"Solving murders or making donuts?" she asked me.

"Well, since the donuts are already made, I can't very well do that," I answered as I started wiping down the tables and putting the chairs up so I could sweep.

"Suzanne Hart, would you stop for one second and give me your full and undivided attention?"

I did as she asked and stood there, waiting for her to say what she had to say. After a few seconds, I asked her, "Exactly how long am I supposed to wait?"

"I want to know what you are doing about Samantha Peterson's murder," she said.

"The police think it's all wrapped up. Haven't you heard the news?"

She scoffed. "Do you honestly think that little sprite of a man had the audacity to kill his boss?"

"I never said it was *my* theory. So, you've heard about Gray's suicide and confession."

"Alleged confession. It all seems a bit too convenient to me, and I'm not the only one in town who thinks our police chief is trying to get a quick solution to quash the rumors that a killer is loose in April Springs. Again."

"I thought Gray's death and confession were supposed to be some kind of secret," I said as I started working again. I couldn't afford to just stand there, and if Gabby wanted to chat, she was going to have to live with my divided attention.

"Evidently, a member of the police force enjoys feeling important," Gabby said. "It's all over town, though the more discerning of us don't believe it."

"I'm not sure what you think I can do about it," I told her as I started running my register report. I knew I needed a more modern version of the current cash register that I'd been using forever, but I didn't have the budget for it, and besides, it was good enough for my needs.

"Suzanne, you have proven yourself to be superior to the police in every way when it comes to investigating murder," Gabby said.

"Hang on a second. Was that a compliment? I'm not sure. How about repeating it?" I asked her with a grin.

"I will do no such thing."

"I didn't think you would, but it was worth a try," I answered. "And thank you. I appreciate you saying that."

"It's a fact. There's no reason to get sentimental about it," she said. "Is there any way I can help you in your investigation?"

I stopped what I was doing. "Gabby, I was under the impression you weren't a big fan of Samantha's."

"I wasn't particularly fond of her. Why do you ask?"

"Why do you care if I solve this case or not then?" If she'd had a personal interest in it, I could maybe understand her behavior, but I just didn't get it.

"She was a strong, competent woman who made her share of enemies by simply doing her job. Does that description sound familiar to you?"

"You mean you can relate to her?" I asked.

"We both can!" she snapped. "If someone decides it's time to start killing strong women in town, we're both no doubt at the top of the list."

"Momma would be too," I added.

"That should give you even more incentive to solve this," she said. "Now, who are your suspects so far?"

I didn't even hesitate answering her question. "That's none of your business."

It was blunt, honest, and direct, three things that Gabby claimed to admire. It would be interesting to see how she felt about those qualities being directed straight back at her.

"That's fair," she said, "but then, strictly speaking, it's none of yours, either, and yet here you are, digging into it as though it were."

"I never admitted I was investigating Samantha Peterson's murder," I told her.

"You never denied it either. Let's not play games, Suzanne." After a moment's pause, she added, "What could it hurt to talk about it with me? I won't repeat what you tell me. You have my word."

I knew I could trust her if she gave me her word, but that wasn't the only reason I was reticent about sharing what I knew so far with her. "Gabby, it's not as easy to deal with as it may seem."

"I'm a grown woman. I can handle it."

"I don't mean that the details of the murder are unsettling. I'm talking about looking at our neighbors and friends as potential killers. Once you start considering the possibility that someone you know could be a killer, it changes the way you look at them forever, whether they turn out to be guilty or not."

Gabby started to say something then paused a moment before speaking. "I never considered that possibility," she admitted, "but if you can do it, then so can I."

"You're not going to let go of this, are you?" I asked as I studied the determined expression she sported.

"What do you think?"

"That you are *almost* as stubborn as I am and that you aren't going to just drop it until your curiosity is satisfied," I said.

"I'm taking that as a compliment," Gabby replied.

"Good, because that's how I meant it." I finally decided that it wouldn't hurt to discuss what Trish and I had learned so far with Gabby. I'd often used Jake, Grace, Momma, and even Phillip as sounding boards in the past. Why not Gabby? "We have it narrowed down to five suspects," I admitted, silently deleting Gray's name from the list. Then again, what if the police chief's theory was right, and it was exactly as it seemed? "Make that six."

"Are you going to stay with that number, or do you wish to add more?" Gabby asked archly.

"Six," I reaffirmed.

"Tell me about them," Gabby said as she took a seat at one of our sofas. I'd just swept under it, so there was no need for her to move, and as long as she was fine with me continuing to shut Donut Hearts down for the day, I wouldn't mind telling her what we knew so far.

"Well, Gray Blackhurst is still on my list, though I'm still not convinced that he killed himself out of remorse. Goodness knows he had reason enough to hate his boss, and truth be told, most times, the simplest answer is the best one. I heard from a pretty unreliable source that she was about to fire him, but I'm taking that with more than a grain of salt."

"That's all well and good, as long as he's not your *only* suspect," Gabby said.

"Not even close," I admitted. At least the kitchen was mostly clean. I had a few dozen donuts left over from the day's sales that I boxed up, and then I put the sheets they'd been on in the kitchen.

"Where are you going, Suzanne?"

"Feel free to come into the kitchen with me, Gabby. I've got to finish these up before the report is done."

"I thought Emma helped you every day," Gabby said.

"She does, but she has a day off during the week, since she and her mother run the place the two days I'm not here."

"And this is her day off?" Gabby asked, pushing harder.

"No. I let her go early." I wasn't about to get into why I'd done it. The whole town might know that the police thought the case was wrapped up, but as far as I knew, nobody was aware of the fact that I'd helped the chief find the password that wrapped things up for them.

"She leads a busy life these days, doesn't she?" Gabby asked.

"We all do," I said, not wanting to get into that at all.

When Gabby realized that I wasn't about to expand on that, she moved back to the case as she followed me into the kitchen and leaned against the wall. "If Gray didn't do it, then who else might have?"

"Well, they had to have come by Donut Hearts yesterday in order to steal the murder weapon," I said. "That limits the field of suspects somewhat."

"I was here," Gabby reminded me. "Am I on that list?"

"No, I saw the strawberry cast iron donut after you left, so I marked you off my list," I told her with a level stare.

"I actually was a suspect at one time?" she asked. The odd thing was that I couldn't tell if that pleased or angered her.

"*Everybody* was a suspect in the beginning," I told her.

"But surely you don't think I'm capable of murder," Gabby said a bit tersely.

"If I've learned anything over the past few years, it's that given the right circumstances, *nobody* is immune to a killing impulse," I told her. "Do you really want to know more about why I feel that way?"

"No," Gabby said, cutting off that diversion. "Go on."

"The list we've been able to come up with..."

She cut me off. "We? I understood that Grace and Jake were both out of town, though not together, of course."

"Of course," I said.

"That leaves your mother and stepfather, but I haven't seen either one of them hanging around the donut shop."

"Trish is working on it with me," I admitted.

"Trish Granger, from the Boxcar?" Gabby asked me a bit incredulously.

"Yes, Trish Granger from the Boxcar. Why are you so surprised?"

"Isn't her personality a bit...forceful for investigating?" Gabby asked me. "Trish has a habit of saying whatever comes to her mind. I would think that might impede people's interest in talking to you."

"She has her strengths too," I said, defending my friend.

"I wasn't criticizing her," Gabby replied quickly. "In fact, that's one of the traits I admire most about her. I'm still waiting for that list, Suzanne."

"Well, if you'd quit interrupting and let me talk, you might hear it," I snapped, perhaps a bit harder than I needed to, but sometimes, that was what it took to get Gabby's attention.

"Point taken," she said. If she was offended by my remark, she certainly didn't show it.

I was about to apologize when I realized that would be precisely the wrong thing to do. Gabby liked it when people didn't tiptoe around her, or at least she claimed to. Saying I was sorry at that point would just make me look weak in her eyes, something that I didn't want, though why it mattered to me I couldn't really say.

"I'll give you our list first, and if you really must know, we can go over motives after," I told her. "How does that sound to you?"

"Whatever you'd like," she replied.

At least I'd gotten her attention. "Very well. We are looking at Gunther Peale, Thompson Smythe, Dr. Zoey Hicks, and Luke Davenport."

Gabby frowned for a moment. "You said you suspected six people earlier, and if we add Gray Blackhurst to your list, that makes just five. Don't hold out on me, Suzanne."

I had left the mayor's name off, whether by accident or on purpose, and I knew it. There was something so final about naming George Morris as a suspect that bothered me. Then again, I couldn't just leave him off because he was my friend.

"George Morris," I said reluctantly.

Gabby smiled. "I thought so."

"Why are you so happy about that?" I asked her. "He's a good friend of mine, you know."

"Mine too, though you might find that hard to believe," Gabby said, "but he had more motive than anyone else to wish to harm Samantha Peterson. She was his rival, and though our mayor may protest that he'd like nothing more than to walk away from his job, we both know that he's lying whenever he says it. He's grown into the role, and it's become a part of him."

It was true, though I'd never actually put the thought out there. "I still don't think he did it," I added a bit petulantly.

"Neither do I," Gabby said.

"Really?"

"No, if the mayor were going to kill her, he would have done it with his bare hands," Gabby said a bit proudly. "I can't see him hitting her with a donut."

"It was a cast iron one," I protested, though why I felt the need to do so was beyond me even as I was saying it.

"Still, George doesn't fit that particular profile. I must say, a few other names surprise me."

"Don't tell me you don't think Zoey Hicks is capable of murder just because she's pretty, do you?"

"Nonsense. I can see her as a killer, but wouldn't she use some medical device, say, poison, to do it? Blunt-force trauma doesn't seem to match her personality."

"She was threatened by Samantha's obsession with Luke," I explained. "He dumped Samantha after he won that money in the lottery, and she wasn't going away quietly. I heard Zoey say that she'd take care of Samantha in my shop not an hour before she found the woman dead, or so she claims. Do you still think she didn't do it?"

Gabby looked a bit surprised. "I had no idea," she admitted. "That changes everything. If that gives Zoey a motive, how about Luke?"

"We think Samantha could have attacked him verbally about dumping her for Zoey, and he fought back," I said.

"So, they both belong on the list, as well as the mayor, whether we like it or not, but one of the names on your roster simply doesn't belong."

"Why, because you know Gunther and Thompson?" I asked her. "Gabby, they both had motive when Samantha disqualified them from the scavenger hunt, they separated at some point before the murder, and though Thompson claims that Gunther alibis him, Gunther himself denies it."

"As well he should," Gabby said.

"Why is that?"

"There's something you don't know," Gabby said.

"As you've been more than happy to point out on more than one occasion, what I don't know could fill an ocean, but what in particular are you talking about now?"

"Gunther couldn't have done it," Gabby answered, although it was clear that it pained her to do so.

"And why is that?"

"Because he was with me," she admitted, something that caught me completely off guard.

Chapter 16

"WHAT DO YOU MEAN HE was with you? After your disastrous brief marriage, I thought you were through with men forever," I told her as I momentarily stopped washing up the last few things I needed to before I drained the water in the sink and moved back out front.

"I thought so too, but lately, Gunther has been trying to convince me otherwise, and I'm afraid I'm starting to waver in my conviction."

"Gabby, there's nothing wrong with being interested in a relationship, but if Gunther was with you, why didn't he just come out and say so?" Another question came to my mind. "In fact, why weren't you two doing the scavenger hunt together?"

"Suzanne Hart, I wouldn't spend a romantic weekend away with a man I hardly know," Gabby chided me.

"Come on, that won't fly, and you know it. You must have known Gunther for forty years."

"Of course I know him, but not *that* way," she said. Was there a hint of blush on her cheeks, or was it just my imagination? "He came to confess that he'd entered the contest with the intent of winning it and buying Thompson's half from him so he could take me with him. I told him he was being ridiculous, but he spent over an hour trying to persuade me that I was wrong."

"And did he?" I asked her, dying of curiosity.

"I hardly see how that's relevant to your investigation," Gabby told me tersely.

"It isn't, but it is as your friend," I told her honestly.

She softened for just a moment as she answered, "I'm not sure."

"Gabby, what do you have to lose? Gunther's a good guy, and we both know that you could do a lot worse."

"And have," she added with more than a hint of regret in her voice.

"It's like they say on those commercials: past performance is no guarantee of future success," I told her. "It's okay to open your heart up to love again."

She bit her lower lip for a moment before answering. "Suzanne, I appreciate your concern, and you know that I love you, but I don't care to discuss it anymore. Is that all right with you?"

"Perfectly," I answered, "but if you ever need to talk, I'm here."

"Where else would you be?" she asked me, though her softened expression told me that she appreciated my offer.

"I don't get one thing. If Gunther was with you, why did Thompson tell me that the two men were together?"

"I'm afraid you'll have to ask him that yourself," Gabby replied.

"Oh, I'm going to, believe you me," I said as I looked around the back. The kitchen was now clean, so all I had left to do was check my report and balance the register till.

As I headed for the front again, Gabby asked, "Are you going to approach Thompson now, without anyone backing you up? If Trish can't come with you, I suppose I could."

I knew what she was offering, and it touched me that she didn't want me to approach a possible killer alone. "Thanks, but I need to finish up here first," I told her. "After I run my report and take my deposit to the bank, I'll go talk to him."

"With Trish," Gabby insisted.

"Yes, with Trish," I answered firmly.

"Then I'll leave you to it, as I see your partner in crime approaching," Gabby commented as she pointed out the front window.

Sure enough, Trish was walking purposefully toward Donut Hearts. It appeared she was lost in thought about something, and when she spotted Gabby inside, she literally stopped in her tracks. I let my friend out and motioned Trish inside before stepping outside briefly to have one more moment alone with Gabby.

"Thanks for checking in with me," I told her as I leaned against the open door.

"Of course," she said brusquely, no doubt some of which was motivated by Trish's near presence. Any tenderness I'd seen in her earlier was now gone, but I knew that it had been there, and that was all that counted. "Keep me posted, Suzanne, and watch your step."

"Always," I told her with a smile, and then she headed off for her gently used clothing store next door. It was good to have her back, a presence in my life again, though there had been times in the not-so-far-away past that the thought would have shocked the socks off me.

People change though, and that went for both Gabby and me.

It was a good reminder that progress was neither a good or a bad thing.

It simply was, and the only hard and true fact was that nothing stayed the same forever.

"What was that all about?" Trish asked me as I rejoined her inside Donut Hearts.

"Gabby stopped in to see how things were going," I told her as I pulled up the report and checked my totals.

"With the donut shop?" Trish asked.

"With our investigation," I admitted.

"You didn't share what we've learned with her, did you?" My friend looked a bit disturbed by the prospect, but I wasn't about to lie to her.

"As a matter of fact, I did."

"Why, Suzanne? Gabby isn't exactly what you'd call circumspect," Trish complained.

Said the kettle to the pot, I thought but did not voice. "Actually, she was a big help."

"How so?"

"She took Gunther Peale's name off our list of suspects," I said as I totaled up the drawer's contents. It was one of those glorious days when everything balanced out to the penny, which was a bit rarer than I was willing to admit.

"How did she do that?"

I wasn't about to divulge Gabby's full confession, not even to Trish. "Believe me. He's in the clear."

"I'd still like to know how you can be so sure," Trish pushed.

"Do you trust me?"

"You know that I do," she answered with a bit of a pout.

"Then take it as fact, and let's move on," I told her. Gabby's story was not mine to tell, and I wasn't about to say anything I didn't have to.

"Just because I trust *you* doesn't mean that I trust *Gabby*," Trish said a bit reluctantly.

"Feel free to ask her yourself, then," I told her as I finished up my deposit and got it ready for the bank.

The prospect of bearding Gabby in her own den was apparently too much for even Trish, which I thought it might be. Gabby could be fierce about her privacy when it suited her, and I couldn't imagine anything more personal than what she'd shared with me earlier. "I believe you," Trish answered simply, ending that particular line of inquiry. "That brings up a new question, though. Why would Thompson Smythe lie to us?"

"We need to find that out, don't we?" I asked her. "After we stop by the bank and make a deposit, we can track him down and ask him ourselves."

"That sounds like a plan," Trish said, and then we both heard my stomach growl. "Was that you?"

"I'm hungry, Trish."

"There are donuts in those two boxes, aren't there?" she asked as she pointed to the counter.

"Frankly, I'm in the mood for something a bit more substantial, but I know you don't want to go by the Boxcar, so I'll be okay."

"What makes you think that?" she asked me.

"Well, you wouldn't want Hilda and Gladys to think you were spying on them, would you?"

"I can't help what they think, but we both have to eat, and where else is there to go?" Trish asked me. "I'm sure not going to that Hot Dog Heaven food cart. Come on."

"So, just to get this straight, we're going there to eat, not to check up on your employees to see how they are handling things in your absence?" I asked with a grin.

"Hey, two birds and all of that," Trish said with a smile of her own. "Come on. Let's go. Tell you what. Why don't we eat first and then go by the bank?"

"No thanks. This may not be much to most folks," I said as I held the deposit bag up, "but I'd feel it if it were lost or stolen. Surely you can wait five minutes to see how the ladies are doing."

"Fine, have it your way," Trish said. She got into the Jeep beside me after I'd locked the donut shop up for the day.

A part of me wanted to go straight to Thompson Smythe's and ask him why he'd lied to us, but it was going to have to wait.

It needed to be business first, and then lunch.

Only after those things were taken care of would I be ready to tackle someone I'd known a very long time who might in fact turn out to be a killer.

"Exactly how long *was* the line inside?" Trish asked me as I got back to the Jeep after making my deposit at the bank.

"About normal," I told her. "Sorry for the inconvenience of making you wait out here for me. I left the engine running so you could stay warm, but you could have always come inside with me."

"I'm the one who's sorry. I shouldn't be complaining, but I'm raring to go."

"To go eat, right?" I asked as my stomach growled a little.

"Yeah. That's exactly what I meant," she said with the hint of a grin. "I *would* like to check out the Boxcar and see how the ladies are doing."

"I'm sure they're doing fine," I told her as I drove over to her diner.

"That's what bothers me. Doesn't it upset you that someone else is running Donut Hearts two days a week when you're not there?"

"It did a little, at least at first, but I've gotten used to it. The truth is that it's nice having some time off," I said, though my voice trailed a bit at the end.

"But," Trish said.

"No buts," I replied quickly.

"Suzanne Hart, I've known you for donkey years. I can hear a 'but' in your conversation even if nobody else can."

I shrugged. "When we're busy and pulling in lots of money, it's nice to have the break, but during the slow weeks, even months, it spreads things a little thin splitting the profits with Emma and Sharon." I'd felt that growing for some time, but up until that point, I hadn't said it aloud to anyone else. It felt good airing it, even though it changed nothing.

"You split them right down the middle, even when you're in charge?" she asked me incredulously.

"No. Of course not. We add up the totals every day they work in my place, deduct expenses, and then split the profits. The rest of the time, Emma is making her regular salary. What's your arrangement with Hilda and Gladys?"

"I'm not giving them anything extra at all," she admitted as she frowned for a second. "That's not really fair of me, is it?"

"You don't have to split your profits with them, but it might be nice to give them each a small bonus," I told her.

"How much is enough? I don't want to insult them, but I also don't want them to expect a lot if we try this again."

"That's entirely up to you," I said. "I have enough trouble dealing with Donut Hearts. You're on your own with the Boxcar Grill."

"Thanks so much for your help," she said, the sarcasm oozing from her voice.

"Hey, what are friends for?" I asked with a laugh.

"I don't know, but I hear it's nice having some. I'll have to get some myself someday," she answered, though she was grinning as she spoke.

"That's the spirit. One can always hope," I said as I pulled into the Boxcar's parking lot. "It looks like business hasn't slackened off any." The lot was fairly full, especially since it was before noon.

"What if nobody has even noticed that I'm gone?" Trish asked me.

I glanced over at her to see if she was joking, but to my surprise, she was dead serious.

"They'll notice, even if they don't say anything. Your customers love you, Trish. You don't have anything to worry about."

"I hope you're right," she said, some of the angst that was in her voice earlier now eased.

"Come on. There's only one way to find out," I said as we headed up the steps to the front door.

"Trish," the crowd called out almost in unison as we walked inside. Hilda was one of the people who looked sincerely happy to see her, and I could see the remaining tension fall away from Trish's shoulders.

"Hey, everybody," Trish said with a grin.

"I'm here too, you know," I said to a few people.

I got a feeble hello of my own, but I wasn't about to take it personally.

"How are things going?" Trish asked Hilda.

"Fine. Okay. All right, I guess," she said.

"Pick one and try that again," Trish told her.

"Do you have a second? I need to ask you about a few things," Hilda said.

"Absolutely," Trish answered, clearly pleased to be needed. "Suzanne, see if you can find us a table. I'll be right there."

"Will do. When you come, grab a couple of sweet teas and whatever the day's special is, would you?"

"I'm not working here at the moment, remember?" she asked.

"I do, but I also remember that I'm hungry, and nobody wants to see that."

"I can't argue with that," Trish said with a shrug. "I'll be there soon."

I looked around and found one table that had only a single occupant. Normally, I wouldn't have hesitated to go over and ask if Trish and I could join him, but from the way the mayor was avoiding eye contact with me, it was clear he wasn't in the mood for company.

That was just too bad.

I had some things to talk about with him, and as uncomfortable as that might be, the conversation had to happen, and sooner rather than later. Doing my best to steel my nerve, I walked over and stood in front of him, so close that he had no choice but to look me in the eye.

"What?" George said a bit grumpily. There was none of the mayoral charm he'd developed since taking office. This was the curmudgeon I'd known before all of that.

Thankfully, I'd never been put off by it before, and I certainly wasn't about to start now. "We need to talk. Mind if I sit?"

"I'd kind of like to be alone," George said as I sat down anyway.

"Well, you keep wishing for things, and maybe someday one of them will come true," I answered with the phoniest smile in my repertoire.

Chapter 17

"I WAS JUST LEAVING, anyway," the mayor replied as he started to get up, though clearly his meal had just been delivered. Either that or he'd lost his appetite, and given the circumstances, it was not hard to imagine why.

"Sit down, George," I said in the most commanding voice I had.

"What did you just say to me, Suzanne? I know you're not giving me orders." His voice was stern, and he was clearly angry about me telling him what to do.

"You heard me. We need to talk. You might not care about what happens, but I do. We've been friends for too long for me to baby you. You can bull your way out of here, and I can't stop you, but doesn't it make more sense to sit there and help me clear your name?"

"It's too late. It doesn't matter if I have an alibi or not; people have already made up their minds that I killed her," he said a bit sullenly.

"How is the mayor so far out of the loop?" I asked him.

"What are you talking about?" George looked seriously confused by my question.

"Have you not spoken to your chief of police today?"

"He's left me half a dozen voicemails, but I've been ignoring him, along with everyone else," the mayor admitted.

"Chief Grant believes the case is wrapped up, and here's a bit of good news: he doesn't think you did it."

"What are you talking about, Suzanne?" the mayor asked me.

"The prevailing theory is that Gray Blackhurst killed himself last night, and there was a confession on his computer that he killed Samantha Peterson," I told him.

"But you don't believe it, do you?" George asked me. The man knew me too well.

"I do not," I said, "and I can't imagine the chief will stick with that theory very long, no matter how convenient it might be to believe it. We've got some time to figure out what really happened in the meantime, and I for one am not going to waste a second of it."

"'We' as in you and me?" he asked. "I thought you and Trish were working this case."

"We are, and even if we weren't, you *can't* help."

"Why not?" George asked me. He knew the answer to that as well as I did, but he was going to make me say it.

"Because you're still on my list of suspects," I told him, meeting his gaze with one of my own.

To my surprise, that made him smile.

"I'm sorry, did I just say something funny that I'm unaware of?" I asked.

"I *need* to be on that list," George said. "I had motive, means, and opportunity. You'd be a fool not to think I might have done it, and you are many things, Suzanne Hart, but you're no fool."

"Thanks for that," I said softly. "We can't do anything about the motive or the means, but it would be great if we had an alibi for you. You said you came back to your office after you two fought, but I never heard if anyone might have seen you there."

"I had people in and out up until I learned about what happened to Samantha, but since I never heard the exact time of death, I couldn't say for sure," the mayor said. "Do you know approximately when she was murdered?"

After I told him, he frowned. "Really? I thought it was much later than that."

"No, we've been able to pinpoint it fairly closely," I told him. "Why, does that matter?"

"As a matter of fact, it does," he said as he looked around the crowded dining room. He found the person he was looking for and called out, "Hannahlee, do you have a second?"

The new employee at city hall came hurrying over to the mayor, leaving her lunch companions watching her intently. They all worked together at city hall, and I had to wonder if there was soon going to be a new round of gossip about the mayor and the pretty new receptionist. "I'm sorry I left my station, but there was no one to ask, and I had to eat lunch," she said, apologizing before George could get a word in edgewise.

"I'm not worried about you taking your lunch hour," George said. "What were you doing yesterday morning from ten to eleven?"

She looked confused. "I was with you in your office. Don't you remember?" She looked a bit concerned, as if it were possible that the mayor had already forgotten about their meeting.

He ignored her question. "And did I ever leave your presence, or you mine, at any time during that meeting?"

"No. What's going on? Should I be concerned, Mayor Morris?"

George looked as though he wanted to kiss her, which would certainly have fueled the rumors that were already no doubt beginning. "Quite the contrary. Why don't you take the rest of the day off? You earned it."

Hannahlee looked back at her colleagues before answering. "Thanks for the generous offer, but if it's all the same to you, I think I'll go back to work after I finish eating."

"That's fine with me," George said. "Go on. You can get back to your lunch. And thank you."

"You're welcome, I guess," she said as she started back to her table. I could see a thousand questions in the eyes of the dining companions she'd just left, so I decided to help her out of the jam the mayor had unknowingly gotten her into.

"I'll be right back, so don't go anywhere," I told the mayor as I followed Hannahlee to her table.

"Was there something else?" the receptionist asked me as she started to take her seat.

"No, I just wanted to thank you for clearing that up for me. I was going to come over and ask you myself, but you know how the mayor can be."

"Is he all right?" she asked me softly. "My grandfather gets forgetful sometimes. He reminds me of the mayor."

I could see the others deflate as the rumor was clearly quashed, and I wanted more than anything to pass that comment on to George, but I decided to be the bigger person and let it slide. "He's just fine. Again, thank you for helping me. The next time you're in Donut Hearts, the first donut is on me."

"Thanks, but I'm afraid I wouldn't be able to stop with just one," she said.

When I got back to the table, George was frowning at me. "What was that all about?"

"The people at that table clearly thought that you were calling Hannahlee over for something personal, not professional," I said with a grin.

"What? That's ridiculous. I've got a lady friend, thank you very much." George started to get up to go over there when I put a hand on his shoulder.

"Don't worry about it. I took care of it," I said.

"What did you say?" he wanted to know.

"It wasn't so much what I said as it was what Hannahlee told them," I answered, not able to help myself after all.

"She denied it?" he asked.

"In a way," I answered.

"Suzanne," George pushed with that tone of voice that told the world he wasn't messing around.

So I told him. "I thanked her for confirming your alibi, and she asked if you were getting forgetful. Evidently her grandfather has the same problem."

George made a noise that sounded like 'humph,' and I could see that he wasn't pleased with the comparison.

"Bring that ego back in check, big guy," I told him with a smile. "Angelica thinks you're dreamy. Do you honestly need women less than half your age swooning over you, too?"

"Dreamy? Swooning? What did you do, swallow a teen romance movie from the fifties?" George asked gruffly. At least most folks would have thought he was being brusque, but for me, it told me that we were on good ground again.

"I'm just happy I can take your name off my list of suspects," I told him as Trish arrived with our food.

"What did I miss?" she asked as she delivered the teas and plates of goodness. Today, it was some kind of shepherd's pie with a side of cranberry sauce and a homemade roll.

"Suzanne can bring you up to speed," George said as he stood.

"You can still eat with us," I told him, gesturing to his half-eaten entrée.

"No offense, but things just aren't the same since you left, Trish," George said.

"How is that even possible? I've only been gone a few hours," Trish protested.

"Really? It feels like it's been days. Hurry back," George said as he threw a ten-dollar bill down and left us, but not before putting a kindly hand on Trish's shoulder. "You have been sorely missed," he added softly.

As George left the diner, I could see a new pep in his step. He'd been beaten before, but now that he had a solid alibi for the time of the murder, he could clearly move forward. I had a feeling that when the next slate of candidates for mayor appeared, George Morris's name would be among them.

"What did I miss?" Trish asked as she took a bite of the shepherd's pie and then made a face. "George is right. What is that, cumin? Hang on. I'll be right back."

Trish headed for the kitchen again, and I started to wonder if I'd lost my investigating partner. She clearly needed to be a part of the everyday operations at the Boxcar Grill, and I could certainly understand it. It was difficult letting go of control, something that I still struggled with from time to time, even though I knew that Donut Hearts was in good hands whenever I was away.

I ate some of the food, then pushed more around on the plate to make it look as though I'd eaten more than I had, when I saw Trish come out of the kitchen. Instead of heading back to our table, she moved over to the Specials Board and erased the shepherd's pie listing.

I made my way to her and said, "Listen, if you need to stay here, I'll be fine on my own."

"Nonsense," Trish said, though I could see by her expression that was exactly what she wanted to happen. "I told you I'd help you, and I meant it."

"Are you sure?"

"Positive," she said before turning to Hilda. "Do you have this?"

"For now, but hurry back, okay? I learned something very important today."

"What's that?" Trish asked her.

"That I love working behind the scenes, not out front. I don't know how you manage to make it look so easy," Hilda said, the admiration clear in her voice.

"We've both got our strengths and weaknesses," Trish told her. "If I had to do all of the cooking, I'd be out of business in a month."

"Oh, I'd give you at least a year," Hilda answered with a smile.

"It's a month, and we both know it."

"Just hurry back," Hilda answered as Gladys called her from the kitchen, and she darted in back to put out another fire, hopefully a figurative one and not a literal one.

Chapter 18

"WHAT DID I MISS?" TRISH asked me as we got back into my Jeep.

"The mayor has an alibi after all," I told her, bringing her up to speed about Hannahlee and the meeting neither one of them had left the day before.

"So we're down to Dr. Hicks, Thompson Smythe, and Luke Davenport," Trish said. "It should be easy from here on out."

"Do you really think so?" I asked her. "In my experience, the nearer you get to the end, the harder figuring out who did it gets to be."

"My money's on Zoey Hicks," Trish said.

"Really? Why is that?"

"I don't know. She just feels like she did it," Trish replied.

I pulled over to the side of the street and put the Jeep in park. "Stop it."

"Stop what? You're the one who is driving."

"Stop jumping to conclusions, especially without evidence," I told her sternly.

"Okay, okay. I'm sorry," she said. "It was just me thinking out loud."

"Trish, thinking like that, even to yourself, can get you killed. We need to assume that *everyone* we come into contact with is dangerous and might try to kill us."

Trish frowned a moment before answering. "That's kind of a negative way to look at life, isn't it?"

"Welcome to my world," I told her. "Right now, we have to be on guard with all three of our remaining suspects. We can't favor one over another unless we have solid evidence to back it up. We might not be cops, but we still can't rely on hunches and intuition. It's important that we both stay alert when we interview our three last suspects and be ready for the unexpected."

"I hear what you're saying, but it's not as easy as it sounds, is it?" she asked me a bit contritely.

"If it were easy, everybody would be doing it," I said with the hint of a smile, trying to take some of the sting out of my earlier words. I needed to wake her up, but I didn't want to run her off either. She had to find that balance if she was going to be able to keep helping me to the conclusion of this case, one way or the other. We both had to stay on our toes, because the person we suspected the least might turn out to be the killer after all. If I were being honest with myself, I would have said that I wouldn't be upset if Zoey turned out to be the killer after all, but that was due more to the fact that I didn't like the woman than that I believed that she'd committed murder.

"Are we okay, Suzanne?" Trish asked me.

"We're fine," I replied. "Why do you ask?"

"Well, you're clearly deep in thought about something, because we're just sitting here when we have three people we need to reinterview."

"Sorry. I got lost there for a second, but I'm back. Remember, guard up at all times, okay?"

"You've got it, Troop Leader," she said as she saluted me with the Girl Scout salute, something we'd gone through together as kids.

"At ease," I told her with a grin.

At least I knew where I was headed.

We needed to speak with Thompson Smythe and find out why he'd lied to us the day before. I hated the idea of verbally sparring with a retired lawyer, but I really had no choice if I was ever going to get to the bottom of who had murdered Samantha Peterson.

I was nearly there when my cell phone rang. Could it be Jake checking in or maybe Momma or Phillip with news of their own? Was Grace back in town early, ready to pitch in once she heard about the murder? I handed my phone to Trish. "Who is it?"

She took it and read, "It's Chief Grant. Should I answer it?"

"Hang on," I said as I pulled over yet again and turned off the engine.

She handed me the phone, and I answered. "Hi, Chief."

"Is this a bad time?" he asked me.

"Usually, that's my question for you," I told him. "No, I can talk."

"It took you a while to answer, that's all," the chief explained.

"I was driving. Is there any news about the case, or do you still think Gray Blackhurst did it?" I asked him.

"This isn't about that, at least not directly," he said.

"Okay, you've certainly got my attention."

"I just wanted to let you know that I found the leak," he answered.

"Anybody I know?" I asked, hoping with all of my heart that it wasn't Darby or even Rick.

"It's a new hire who's only been with me a week," he explained. "You might not have even met him yet."

"And he's already leaking information to the press?" I asked. "Did you fire him?"

"Oh, no," Chief Grant said with a hint of joy in his voice. "That would have been too easy."

"For him or for you?" I asked.

"Absolutely for him. I've got him on midnight dispatch duty, and then he's going to supervise the crosswalks for the rest of his probation period. He's got the makings of being a good cop, but not until he learns to keep his mouth shut."

"Wow, you're one of the few people I know whose bite is actually worse than their bark," I told him.

"What's the matter, don't you approve?"

"I never said that," I told him. "I'm glad you figured it out."

"So am I." He paused for a moment, and I could tell he wasn't finished.

I could have prodded him a little, but I knew from experience that wasn't the way to get it out of him. Instead, I just sat there and waited in silence, giving him time to decide to speak first. Trish glanced at me with a curious expression, but I just held up one finger and mouthed the word "Wait" to her.

Sure enough, he finally decided to speak after all. "I'm not entirely sure that you're not right about this case," he said softly. "There's something about it that is starting to feel a bit too convenient to me. Do you know what I mean?"

"I do," I said. "Does that mean you're okay if Trish and I keep digging into this?"

"Yes, but be careful. If Gray did it, all you'd do is anger some people with your questions, but if it was someone else, it could be a lot more dangerous than that."

"We're being careful," I told him. "Thanks, Chief."

"For?"

"The information and the confession," I told him.

He didn't answer, he just hung up, which I decided to take as a "you're welcome," whether he meant it to be that or not.

"Do you mind telling me what that was all about?" Trish asked me as I started my Jeep yet again and finished driving the last two hundred feet to Thompson Smythe's house.

"It wasn't about the murder investigation," I told her. "Well, at least not entirely."

"Did he give you his blessing for us to keep digging?" Trish asked me.

"Let's just say he didn't tell us to STOP," I said, making the last word emphatic enough to match the notes we'd both gotten just that morning.

"We still don't know who left us those little messages, do we?" Trish asked me as I parked in front of Thompson's place.

"No, but I have a hunch that when we figure out who really killed Samantha Peterson and Gray Blackhurst, we'll know."

Trish grinned at me. "I didn't think we were supposed to have hunches."

I had to laugh. "You got me there. Are you ready for this?" I asked as I saw the man in question come out of his front door and stop dead in his tracks when he noticed that we were there, parked in front of his sedan, virtually blocking him in and cutting off any hope he might have had for fast escape.

"It doesn't seem that we have any choice," Trish said as we both opened our doors and confronted someone who might just be a killer.

"I don't have time for your foolishness, ladies," Thompson said tersely before either one of us could get a word out. "Please move your vehicle. I have somewhere I need to be."

"I'd be glad to move," I said, not meaning it at all. "What's the rush though? You're not leaving town, are you?"

He looked at me angrily. "What I do or do not do is frankly none of your business."

"I just thought with you being a suspect in Samantha Peterson's murder, you might want to stay close."

That caught his attention. "I'm no more a suspect than you are, Ms. Hart."

It had always been Suzanne before, but suddenly he'd gotten all formal on me. I took that as a good sign that I was getting his attention. "I don't have motive, means, or opportunity."

"And you're claiming that I do? It was your donut that killed the woman, not mine!"

He was getting a little upset with me, which was fine. Maybe I'd be able to break through that normally calm exterior and get somewhere. "That's fair. The police have only my word that someone else took it, but I was at Donut Hearts when the murder happened, whereas you were seen arguing with the murder victim just before she died."

"You forget, I have an alibi," he answered.

"Not so much. We spoke with Gunther again, and he has proof that he was someplace else when you claimed he was with you," Trish said.

"Then they are both mistaken," he answered. "Now, are you going to move that thing, or do I need to call the police and have it removed from my property?"

I made no move to vacate. Instead, I stood my ground and smiled. "Call the police. That's a wonderful idea. I'd love to hear you deny what you told us earlier to them."

That brought the retired attorney up short. It was clear he hadn't expected me to call his bluff. "Fine. Let's get this over with. I was covering for Gunther."

"Why would you feel the need to do that?" Trish asked him, which was a question that was on my lips as well.

"I served as an attorney for forty-two years," he said, "whereas he made a living with his brute strength. It's obvious he is a more likely killer than I would ever be, so I decided to cover for him."

"So you lied?" I asked him softly.

"To you, not the police," he reminded me.

"That still counts as lying," Trish replied angrily.

"Not to me it doesn't. If you don't like it, I suggest you take your complaints up with someone else, because frankly, I don't care."

I decided to try a different tack. "So, what are you going to tell them when they ask you for an alibi?"

"They won't. I have it on good authority that the case has been solved. Why are you two even here? It's over, or hadn't you heard? Go home."

He looked a little too smug for my taste with that. "It's not as finished as you might think. The police are reexamining their evidence even as we speak, and that means they'll be knocking on your door again soon." It was hopeful at best, a lie at worst, but I didn't really have any choice. Now it was my turn to bluff. "I repeat, what are you going to tell them?"

"When and if they come, I'll tell them the truth, but you two will get nothing more from me." He pulled out his phone and started to dial.

I didn't know if he was bluffing or not, but I didn't have much choice. I had no official standing in the case, and I couldn't force the man to tell me anything. "Fine. We're leaving," I said.

"But, Suzanne, he never answered your question," Trish protested.

"We'll take it up again later," I told her.

"You can ask all you want, but as I just said, I won't be answering any more questions from you two. Good day."

"Good day to you," I said as I got in my Jeep. Trish joined me, and I backed up to let Thompson leave.

"We're giving up too easily," Trish said curtly.

"Who said we were giving up?" I asked her with a grin.

"Suzanne, what are you up to?"

"I don't know about you, but I'm kind of curious about what's got him in such a rush. Shall we follow him and see?"

"You sneaky devil, you," she said with her full approval. "That sounds like a plan."

I pulled away from Thompson's house and drove around the block, slowing down to catch sight of his new destination.

I was guessing that he'd drive toward Union Square, so I found a nearby parking lot and pulled in to wait as I pointed in that direction.

Only he ended up going toward Maple Hollow instead.

I'd started to turn around to follow him when a cement truck lumbered by, stopping right in front of the exit as it broke down. I tried to get around him, but it was too tight a squeeze. I finally managed to maneuver the Jeep and get it pointed in the right direction, but by then, I was too late.

Thompson Smythe was gone.

I'd lost him.

Chapter 19

"WHAT DO WE DO NOW?" Trish asked me as she realized that we'd failed in our basic objective.

"Well, we have two suspects left," I told her. "Let's go see if we can find Zoey Hicks and Luke Davenport."

"Zoey could be at the hospital," Trish suggested, "and seeing how we're pointing in that direction anyway, let's try there first."

"It's as good an idea as any. Sorry I messed up," I told her as I drove toward the hospital.

"Suzanne, you didn't make that cement truck break down, and where else were you going to be able to wait to follow Thompson? It was just plain bad luck, that's all."

"Maybe, but we really can't afford to lose sight of him like that," I answered.

"Hey, we aren't cops. Don't be so hard on yourself."

"Trish, I appreciate the sentiment, but this could be important. Where was he going in such a hurry? Did he lose us on purpose, or was it just a bad break? And why won't he tell us his alibi, especially after getting caught lying to us before?"

"Hey, he's a lawyer. You can't expect him to roll over and cooperate just because we ask him to. I can't believe more people don't tell you to go bark at the moon when you press them with questions. This is a lot harder than I thought it would be."

"And it gets harder every time," I said as I pulled in. "Maybe the breaks are evening out."

"What do you mean?"

"There's Dr. Zoey Hicks just leaving the hospital," I said as I pointed in the direction I was suddenly driving. "We might have just caught a break after all."

"Hello, Suzanne, Trish," the doctor said a bit sadly after we got out and approached her.

It was clear that something was bothering her, and I couldn't help myself but ask her why. My humanity was more important that investigating a murder, at least at that moment. "Is something wrong?"

"I just finished the autopsy on Gray Blackhurst," she said with a frown. "The police asked me to rush it. I sincerely doubt he meant to kill himself, but if that was his goal, he was a ripping success at it."

"So, you don't think it was suicide or even possibly murder?" I asked her.

"What an odd question. Why do you ask?" she posed.

"I'm just wondering if someone could have killed him and made it look as though it was his own doing," I explained.

"I doubt it. That might work in bad movies, but it didn't feel that way to me."

"How are you officially ruling, then?" I asked her.

"Accidental death," she answered.

"So you don't think there's a chance it was homicide," I pushed her.

"Not unless someone held a gun to his head and *made* him take those pills. As far as I'm concerned, it was either accidental or deliberate, but whatever happened, it was from Gray Blackhurst's actions and no one else's."

"Thank you for sharing that with us," I told her, forgetting for a moment why we had hunted her down in the first place.

Trish clearly hadn't. "You first told us that Luke went for coffee when you found Samantha's body, is that right?"

"That's what I said," she answered.

"That's funny, because Luke told us you weren't together because he broke up with you," Trish pushed.

Zoey frowned a moment before speaking. "Fine. He dumped me. Happy?"

I stepped between them. "We're not prying for no reason. We're just trying to make sense of what happened. Now more than ever, we don't buy the idea that Gray killed Samantha and then took his own life."

"It's within the realm of possibility," Dr. Hicks said. "Why don't you believe it?"

"I read the note. It seems out of character for him."

"There was a note? Well, he certainly wouldn't have written one if he died of an accidental overdose, would he? Maybe I need to change my findings. The police chief didn't tell me about finding a suicide note."

"Hold off on filing that report for a bit, would you?" I asked.

"Why should I?"

"I'd rather Samantha's real killer think they got away with it for the moment," I answered.

Zoey shivered. "I have devoted my life to saving people. I can't understand how *anyone* could take someone else's life."

"People lash out all the time, especially when they're angry," I reminded her.

The nuance wasn't lost on Dr. Hicks. "Hang on a second. Do you honestly think *I* killed Samantha because Luke dumped me? What would be the motive for that? He broke up with me before we even got to the gazebo." She paused and then said, "It was almost as though he planned it to happen that way."

"How so?" I asked her.

She seemed to be working it out as she went. "I *thought* it felt staged. What if dumping me was just an excuse Luke was using to be alone so he could get rid of her himself?"

"I don't follow," I said. "If you weren't around and he wasn't interested in dating Samantha anyway, why would he want her dead?"

"You don't know, do you?" Dr. Hicks asked. "It doesn't surprise me. He didn't tell anybody about it but me, and she promised to be quiet as well, as long as he followed through with his promise."

"What are you talking about?" I asked her, confused by what was going on.

"He and Samantha bought that lottery ticket together. He claimed that he won on another, separate ticket, and she was threatening to take him to court to get her half of the money he won."

"When did you learn that?"

"Right after we left your donut shop," she said angrily. "I pushed him about why Samantha was so obsessed with him, and he confessed the truth: that he'd cheated her after all. I demanded that he do the right thing, and he dumped me because of it! Honestly, he did me a favor. I don't want to be with someone I can't trust."

Trish was clearly about to ask her a follow-up question when the doctor's pager went off. "I've got to go," she said as she raced back toward the building. "It's an emergency."

"Well, that certainly puts a new spin on things," I said after she was gone.

"Luke did it, didn't he?" Trish asked me.

"We don't know that, but it's looking more likely than it was before," I admitted. "Don't forget Thompson. He was up to something, that much is clear. I don't buy for one second that he was lying to protect Gunther Peale."

"I don't either," Trish said.

"Hey, I just had a wild thought."

"What's that?" she asked.

"Bear with me for a second. What if Samantha talked Thompson into coming out of retirement to represent her in her case against Luke?" I asked.

"Would he do that?"

"If the fee was high enough, why wouldn't he?" I asked. "That might tie Thompson into the case more than we realized."

Trish looked confused. "Nothing is turning out to be what it seemed to be at first, is it?"

"That's the way it happens sometimes. The deeper you dig into things, the more dirt you uncover," I told her.

"There's just one thing I don't get about that scenario. Why would Thompson kill Samantha if she was going to be his golden goose?" Trish asked.

"I don't know," I said after a moment's thought. "Maybe she was going to fire him. Maybe she wanted to get back together with Luke and was just using the case for leverage? Thompson could have seen a big fat contingency fee slipping away, and they could have argued about it. You saw how easily he got upset with us for asking him more questions today. He clearly had *something* to hide. We just didn't know what."

"Does that mean that we're taking Zoey Hicks off our list of suspects?" she asked me.

"I think so," I admitted. "If she had anything to do with Gray's death, I have a feeling we would have seen it in her behavior. In case you haven't noticed, she's not that good at hiding her emotions. It wasn't a murderer telling us about those autopsies, it was a caring human being. I might not be the woman's biggest fan, but I don't think she had anything to do with this case."

"I agree," Trish said, "on all counts. So then that just leaves us with Luke Davenport and Thompson Smythe. But which one?"

"I don't know yet, but that's what we need to find out. Let's go track Luke down and see if we can't get the real story out of him."

"Luke, come out. We know you're here. Your truck is in the driveway. Come on. This won't take long," I said after pounding on the door again and leaning on his doorbell for the third time.

"Suzanne, he might really be gone," Trish said after trying to look through the windows again with no luck. The blackout shades shut out more than sunlight.

They also kept us from peering in.

"If he's gone, then why is his truck still here?" I asked her as I started to walk around the back of the house.

"Maybe he walked wherever he was going," she suggested.

"I doubt it. Luke doesn't seem the walking type to me," I answered.

As we turned the corner, Trish said, "He did it, didn't he?"

"The odds are certainly good," I told her, "but I want to ask him a few more questions before I'm satisfied."

That was when I heard a man say, "You just won't stop, will you, no matter how many notes I leave you?"

And I knew that I'd pushed my luck once too many times as I stared at a gun pointing straight at my heart.

Chapter 20

"THOMPSON, WHAT ARE you doing here?" I asked him as I glanced over at Trish. I had never seen that expression on her face in all of the years I'd known her. She was terrified, and for a second, I was worried that she might be having some kind of seizure.

"Get inside. Both of you," he said as he motioned toward the back door with the gun.

"It's locked," I told him, more worried about Trish at that second than I was about dying.

"Not back here it's not," he answered. "I'm not going to tell you again."

I moved for the door, but I saw that Trish was rooted to the ground as though her feet were buried in cement.

I moved toward her when Thompson barked out, "What do you think you are doing?"

"She's scared," I told him.

"Well, she'd better get over it, or in a second, she's going to be dead. They can't punish me more for three murders than they can for one."

"You mean two or even three, don't you? Luke is probably dead, and you already killed Samantha and Gray," I said as I took Trish's arm and tried to pull her toward the house.

She didn't even seem to realize I was there.

This was bad, really bad.

"I was quite careful about my word choice," Thompson said, and then he looked closely at Trish again. "What's wrong with her? She's going to get you both killed out here if she doesn't snap out of it."

I couldn't bring myself to slap my friend, but I did pinch her arm as hard as I could.

That finally got her attention. "Ouch. Why did you do that?"

"We need to go inside, Trish," I told her as I gestured toward the house.

Her eyes finally unglazed, and I saw her glance over at Thompson, or more importantly, the gun in his hand.

We could both see her start to scream when he shoved the gun hard into my chest. "Make one sound and she's dead."

The breath choked out of Trish at that instant, and so did her budding scream.

"Get her inside, Suzanne. I'm not telling you again," the attorney/murderer demanded.

I grabbed Trish's arm again and pulled her toward the door.

At least she moved with me.

We made quite the train going into Luke's house, with Trish in the lead, me sandwiched between them, and Thompson following close behind. I kept hoping that Luke was alive and somewhere nearby, ready to pounce on the attorney and wrestle the gun out of his hands.

When I walked through the threshold, I saw that hope was in vain.

Luke was sitting in a chair in the middle of the living room, neatly trussed up and gagged.

We wouldn't be getting any help from him after all.

I looked wildly around for something I could use as a weapon, but all I saw were a slew of Luke's tools on the floor. Was there anything there I could use?

I spotted a screwdriver that might make a good weapon, but I couldn't exactly bend down to retrieve it, not with Thompson so close.

I needed a diversion.

Making a silent plea for forgiveness from Trish, I did the only thing I could think to do.

I tripped her.

As she fell, I pretended to try to break her fall, but all the while, I focused on retrieving that screwdriver. It was the slotted kind, so the point was a flat, tapered end. I would have much preferred an awl with a needlepoint, but beggars couldn't be choosers. As I reached down to help Trish up, I slipped the screwdriver up my sleeve, hoping that it didn't fall out before I was ready to use it.

"You two are more trouble than you're worth," the attorney snapped. "Drag those two chairs over to where Luke is."

I knew if we let him truss us up, we would be at his mercy. I needed to act, and quickly.

"The police know we're here," I said in a bold attempt at bluffing.

"I doubt that," Thompson replied.

"But what if I'm right? You can run right now, and who knows? You might even get away with it."

"First of all, I'm not going anywhere, at least not yet. I have some business to conclude first," he added as he gestured to Luke.

"Let us go then, and we'll let you handle whatever you need to do," I said. I figured it was worth a shot.

"No thank you." He glanced at something on the table nearby, and I thought about attacking him while he was distracted, but the only problem was that Trish was standing between us. By the time I got around her and at his throat, at least one of us would most likely be dead. "You might be of use to me after all. I got him to sign already, but a pair of witnesses would seal the deal."

"What are you talking about?" I asked him as I tried to move around Trish. I pretended to be interested in seeing the paper he was looking at, but really, I was trying to get a chance to attack him.

"Stay right where you are," he said as he noticed me moving. "Trish, come over here."

She was back in her daze, and she didn't move.

"Trish," I said loudly, snapping out her name as though I were giving her a command. "This is important."

She came a little out of her fog. "What?"

"She's useless," Thompson said with a frown. "Get over here, Suzanne."

This was my chance. I started toward him when he pointed his gun directly at Trish's heart. "Don't try anything, or she's dead."

I was beaten, and I knew it. I had no trouble risking my own life or even Luke's, but I couldn't put Trish in danger.

It was starting to feel as though Thompson had won after all.

Chapter 21

MAYBE IF I GOT HIM talking, I could get a chance to act. "Why do you need us?"

"I need a witness to sign this document. Luke here has graciously agreed to assign me his lottery winnings in exchange for services rendered." He glanced over at his captive and said jovially, "Isn't that right, Luke?"

Luke shook his head violently.

"He doesn't seem to agree," I said calmly.

"Really? How odd. He just signed the paper agreeing to it," Thompson said.

"I still don't understand why you killed Samantha," I told him. Hopefully, I could distract him long enough to move and not jeopardize Trish's life.

Hopefully.

"She hired me to sue this thief for her half of the winning lottery ticket, but when she found out he was breaking up with the good doctor, she changed her mind and fired me. I tried to convince her that she couldn't trust him, but she wouldn't listen to reason."

So I'd been right with one of my wild guesses, for all the good it did us now. "So you killed her for that?" I asked him.

"No, I merely pointed out a few facts to her about her shortcomings, and she took offense. She came at me, and I had to defend myself, didn't I?"

He had clearly already rationalized killing the woman. "With my cast iron donut? Why did you steal that, anyway? Were you planning this all along?"

"No, that was purely happenstance. I saw it, I liked it, so I slipped it into my pocket. You had three. You didn't need all of them."

"Are you in the habit of stealing from people?" I asked him.

"Lately, I have found myself caring less and less about other people's personal property," he said with a shrug.

"The bookmark Trish spotted. That was hers too, wasn't it?"

The attorney grinned. "What are you going to do, arrest me?"

I decided to let that one go. "So, if you killed Samantha in self-defense, why run away at all?"

"No one would believe me," the attorney said. "I figured Samantha had enough enemies that the list of suspects would be huge, and I was right."

"But why use Gunther as an alibi without at least checking with him first?" I asked. I took the opportunity to glance at Trish.

She hadn't moved. She was clearly back in her own little world of terror. I couldn't fault her for her reaction. Anyone in their right mind would feel the same way.

"I thought the fool would back me up. After all, he needed an alibi as badly as I did."

"Only he already had one," I told him, "so you killed Gray and framed him instead to take the heat off you."

"I did no such thing!" the attorney denied. "The man was already dead when I found him."

Chapter 22

"ARE YOU SAYING *someone else* killed him?" I asked.

"No, it was clearly an accidental overdose," the attorney replied.

"Why were you there in the first place?" I really wanted to know the answer to that question, and if there was a chance I was going to die in the next few minutes, I at least wanted to have my curiosity satisfied.

"Samantha told me that she kept the proof of her share of the winning ticket with her assistant," he explained. "I went by his place to search for it, but there was no answer when I knocked on the door. It wasn't locked, so I decided to look around for myself, only to find the man's body."

"So you wrote the suicide note to lay the blame on him," I finished.

"It was a stroke of brilliance, if I say so myself," he crowed.

"The truth is, it wasn't all *that* brilliant," I corrected him.

"What do you mean?"

"You left the piece of paper with the password on it at the scene," I told him. "I'm the one who found it. That was sloppy. Plus, you never printed out the suicide note, which was clearly written by someone who had never even met Gray Blackhurst. Peace? Really? Those were rookie mistakes too, Counselor."

His expression got cloudy with anger. Good. I was trying to antagonize him to get him to lose focus on Trish for a second or two, even if it meant directing it at me. It would lessen my odds of surviving this mess, but it should increase Trish's.

At least that was my hope.

"That meddlesome police chief came pounding on the front door, and I had to get out of there quickly. I dropped the crumpled password, but I couldn't get the stupid note to print out, so I had to leave in a rush. At least I got the proof I needed, not that I can use it now."

"All you had to do was turn the printer on, and the note came right out," I said, scolding him as though he were some kind of idiot.

"I've had enough of you," he snarled as he pulled the gun from Trish and started to point it at me.

It was my moment, and at the last second, I had some help that I hadn't been expecting.

Trish pulled out of her fog long enough to stamp hard on the attorney's foot!

The move caught him off guard, and as he swung the handgun back to her, I acted.

Pulling the screwdriver out of my sleeve, I rushed him.

And with every ounce of energy I had, I plunged it into his chest.

I hadn't been trying to kill him, but what choice did I have?

It was either us or him, and I chose us.

Ten out of ten.

Chapter 23

"IS HE DEAD?" I ASKED the paramedics as they swarmed over the attorney a little later.

"No, you missed his heart, but just barely. He's going to need surgery, but he should make it," Howie said as he and Gert rushed away with the cart.

Luke was still rubbing his hands where he'd been bound so tightly, and he walked over to me as Trish finished giving her statement to Chief Grant. I'd already told him what had happened the moment he arrived after our call, but I couldn't fault him for being thorough.

"You saved me," he said. "Thank you."

"I was saving Trish and me," I told him blankly. "You just happened to be here too."

That caught him by surprise. "Listen, I know I screwed up, but I'm going to make it right. As soon as I get out of here, I'm sending Samantha's family her half of the money I won."

"It's too little, too late to do her any good though, isn't it?" I asked dully. It was probably a cruel thing to say, but my filter was off, and I was upset about nearly killing someone, even if he had probably deserved it.

Luke just shrugged and frowned. "It's what I can do right now."

I could see the pain and anguish in his face. I put a hand on his shoulder. "I suppose it's easy enough to understand what you did," I told him. "Most folks would have done the exact same thing given your situation."

"That doesn't make it right though, does it? You wouldn't have cheated someone close to you," he said.

"I'd like to think that I wouldn't, but then again, I've never been put into that situation," I admitted.

"Thanks for that, at least," he said as the chief came.

"I'd like to give you all a ride to the hospital. Let's go."

"I don't need to go," I protested.

"I know that, but I thought you might want to be with Trish," he said gently.

I glanced over at my friend and saw that she was silently weeping. I wasn't even certain that she was aware of it.

"You're right. I do," I said. "Let's go."

"I don't need to go too, do I?" Luke asked.

"I'm not finished with you yet, so I'm not letting you out of my sight," the chief said, the tenderness now gone from his voice.

"I understand," he said.

I was about to defend Luke in whatever way I could when I realized that I had another priority at the moment.

I hurried over to Trish and wrapped my arms around her. "It's okay. We're safe now."

"But we almost died," she muttered through her tears.

"You stepped up though, and I mean that literally," I told her as I stroked her back. "You should be proud of yourself."

"You're the one who put that monster down," Trish whimpered.

"That's the thing though. I don't think he's a monster. He let his bad side get the best of him, and he's going to pay for what he did, but he's not a monster. I reserve that term for the ones who deserve it more than he does."

"Suzanne, no offense, but I can't do this. The next time you need someone to help you with one of these things, skip me and move on to the next person on your list, okay?"

There was a glimmer of the spark I knew and loved in her gaze, and for the first time in the past hour, I started to believe that she was going to come out of this mess okay. "Hopefully, there won't be a next time," I said. "I'm getting tired of getting dragged into these investigations, and if I have any say in the matter, I'm quitting and going back to full-time donut making. It's what I love doing and what I'm good at."

As I said those words, I hoped that they were true. I had experienced more than my share of killers, of close calls and near misses. I knew the odds were running against me, and that it was time to quit while I still could.

I just hoped the world saw it that way too and left me alone.

It was something to wish for, anyway, I thought as I helped get Trish into the police cruiser so we could take her where she could get the care she needed. Her spirit had taken a pounding in Luke Davenport's house, and while I saw signs that she was bouncing back, I knew from experience that she'd wake up from nightmares for some time to come.

It was one of the prices we all paid for digging into murder and one I was sure she hadn't counted on when she'd so glibly offered to help.

Hopefully, someday, someday soon, the nightmares would go away. For both of us.

RECIPES

A Good Basic Donut

This is the first donut recipe I ever created, and I go back to it from time to time when I want something that reminds me of the many delights I've made over the years. This recipe is a good one to start with because there's no yeast involved, no proofing times, and no tricky steps to get a good donut. It's still one of my favorites, and I love making these when it's dreary out and I need something to pick me up. After all, there's nothing like a fresh homemade donut to do the trick, at least as far as I'm concerned!

Ingredients

4 1/2 cups bread flour

1 cup granulated sugar

1 1/2 teaspoon baking soda

1 teaspoon nutmeg

1 teaspoon cinnamon

2 dashes of salt

1 egg, beaten

1/2 cup sour cream

1 cup buttermilk

Peanut oil, enough to fry the donuts in

Directions

Heat the peanut oil to 375°F. It won't hurt to let it simmer once it's up to the proper temperature while you're preparing the donuts.

In a large bowl, sift together the flour, sugar, baking soda, nutmeg, cinnamon, and salt.

Add the beaten egg to the dry mix then add the sour cream and buttermilk to the mixture and stir. The dough should resemble bread dough when you're finished, meaning it shouldn't stick to your hands when you touch it, but it should be moist enough to remain flexible. If it's too dry, add a bit more buttermilk; too moist, add a bit more flour.

Knead the mix lightly then roll out to about 1/4 inch thick.

Use a donut hole cutter or even a water glass to press out donut shapes, reserving the holes for a later frying.

Put 4 to 6 donuts in the heated oil but don't crowd the pot, then fry 2 minutes per side, flipping each time.

Once done, remove each donut to a cooling rack or a plate lined with paper towels to drain.

While they are still warm, brush the tops with glaze, or butter them and then sprinkle with powdered sugar and cinnamon, or simply eat plain.

Makes approximately 1 dozen donuts.

A Good Basic Glaze

There's nothing difficult about this glaze, which I love. It works for just about any sweet treat, and I've been known to put it on more than donuts in the past. Don't ask, so I don't have to lie to you, but take my word for it, it's delicious!

Ingredients

2 cups confectioners' sugar

6 tablespoons milk

1 teaspoon vanilla extract

In a medium bowl, stir together the confectioners' sugar, vanilla extract, and 6 tablespoons milk until smooth.

Dip warm donuts into glaze or drizzle the glaze on top.

My New Best Apple Pie Recipe

My family loves my apple pies. I've been making them for over twenty-five years, and one member of my family still requests it as their "birthday cake" every year! It's perfect when the apples are in season, but the truth is that I make these year-round. In fact, it wouldn't be Thanksgiving or a holiday feast without one.

Recently, I've been playing around with the recipe, trying for even more perfection, and I believe I've found it. Adding some cinnamon and nutmeg to the crumb topping itself takes these pies to a completely different level, so if you're a fan of these spices—and you should be to make these pies—give it a try, but don't forget the vanilla ice cream to go on top!

Ingredients

9-inch deep dish pie crust, premade

Filling

1/2 cup granulated sugar

3 tablespoons flour

1 teaspoon nutmeg

1 teaspoon cinnamon

Dash of salt

5 to 6 cups thinly sliced firm, tart apples (I like to use two or three Granny Smiths and one or two Pink Ladies, but as long as you combine tart apples with sweet ones, you can't go wrong.)

Topping

1 cup flour

1/2 cup brown sugar, packed tightly

1 teaspoon cinnamon

1 teaspoon nutmeg

1/2 cup butter, chilled but not frozen

Directions

Preheat the oven to 425°F.

Peel and core the apples then cut them into thin slices.

In a medium bowl, sift together the sugar, flour, nutmeg, cinnamon, and salt, then stir this mixture into the apples until they are thoroughly coated.

Add the coated apples to the pie shell, stacking them so they form a uniform domed shape.

In a medium bowl, combine flour, brown sugar, cinnamon, and nutmeg.

Cut in the chilled butter, mixing thoroughly. The topping should be crumbly and the butter still in small chunks.

Add this mixture to the top of the pie, then bake on a cookie sheet to catch any errant juices. Bake for 35 to 45 minutes.

NOTE: I loosely tent aluminum foil over the top of the pie after 30 minutes or when the topping is dark golden brown and then bake until a knife slips into the top with some resistance. I like my apples to be a bit crunchy, so you need to judge for yourself how firm you want them. If you like soft apples, don't be afraid to leave the pie in the oven a bit longer, tented, for the full 50 minutes or even longer if needed.

Serves 4 to 6.

The Easiest Donut Recipe You'll Ever See

Calling this a recipe is a stretch, but honestly, these make amazing donuts with very little work on your part. You'll look like a hero serving these! Try some of the glaze listed above, sprinkle them with powdered sugar, or spread on your favorite jam or jelly.

Ingredients

1 can (16 oz.) biscuit dough (I like the sourdough recipe)

Enough peanut oil to fry them

Directions

Put enough peanut oil in a large-bottomed pot to fry the rounds, then heat the oil to 375°F.

Remove the rounds from their can, then use a hole cutter or small glass to cut out the centers of the biscuits.

Fry 2 minutes on each side, turning halfway through, including the donut holes you removed as well.

Drain on paper towels or a wire rack and eat plain, glaze, dust with powdered sugar, or use your favorite jam or jelly as a topping.

Makes 8 donuts and 8 donut holes.

If you enjoy Jessica Beck Mysteries and you would like to be notified when the next book is being released, please visit our website at jessicabeckmysteries.net for valuable information about Jessica's books, and sign up for her new-releases-only mail blast.

Your email address will not be shared, sold, bartered, traded, broadcast, or disclosed in any way. There will be no spam from us, just a friendly reminder when the latest book is being released, and of course, you can drop out at any time.

Other Books by Jessica Beck

The Donut Mysteries
Glazed Murder
Fatally Frosted
Sinister Sprinkles
Evil Éclairs
Tragic Toppings
Killer Crullers
Drop Dead Chocolate
Powdered Peril
Illegally Iced
Deadly Donuts
Assault and Batter
Sweet Suspects
Deep Fried Homicide
Custard Crime
Lemon Larceny
Bad Bites
Old Fashioned Crooks
Dangerous Dough
Troubled Treats
Sugar Coated Sins
Criminal Crumbs
Vanilla Vices
Raspberry Revenge
Fugitive Filling
Devil's Food Defense
Pumpkin Pleas
Floured Felonies
Mixed Malice

A Killer Cake
A Baked Ham
A Bad Egg
A Real Pickle
A Burned Biscuit
The Ghost Cat Cozy Mysteries
Ghost Cat: Midnight Paws
Ghost Cat 2: Bid for Midnight
The Cast Iron Cooking Mysteries
Cast Iron Will
Cast Iron Conviction
Cast Iron Alibi
Cast Iron Motive
Cast Iron Suspicion
Nonfiction
The Donut Mysteries Cookbook